BAKEMONOGATARI

MONSTER TALE

PART 01

NISIOISIN

VERTICAL.

BAKEMONOGATARI
Monster Tale
Part 01

NISIOISIN

Art by VOFAN

Translated by Ko Ransom

VERTICAL.

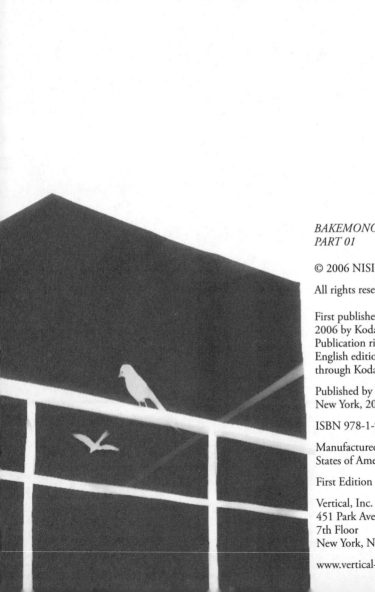

BAKEMONOGATARI,
PART 01

© 2006 NISIOISIN

All rights reserved.

First published in Japan in
2006 by Kodansha Ltd., Tokyo.
Publication rights for this
English edition arranged
through Kodansha Ltd., Tokyo.

Published by Vertical, Inc.,
New York, 2016

ISBN 978-1-942993-88-9

Manufactured in the United
States of America

First Edition

Vertical, Inc.
451 Park Avenue South,
7th Floor
New York, NY 10016

www.vertical-inc.com

CHAPTER ONE
HITAGI CRAB

001

Hitagi Senjogahara occupies the position of "the girl who's always ill" in our class. She's not expected to participate in P.E., of course, and is even allowed to suffer morning and school-wide assemblies in the shade, alone, as a precaution against anemia or something. Though we've been in the same class my first, my second, and this, my third and final year of high school, I've never once seen her engaged in any sort of vigorous activity. She's a regular at the nurse's room, and she arrives late, leaves early, or simply doesn't show up to school because she has to visit her primary care hospital, time and again. To the point where it's rumored in jest that she lives there.

Though "always ill," she is by no means sickly. She's graceful, like her thin lines could snap at a touch, and has this evanescent air, which must be why some of the boys refer to her as "the cloistered princess" half-jokingly, half-seriously. You could say earnestly. That phrase and its connotations aptly describe Senjogahara, I agree.

Senjogahara is always alone reading a book in one corner of the classroom. At times that book is an imposing hardcover, and at others it's a comic that could permanently damage your intellect to judge from its cover design. She seems to be one of those voracious readers. Maybe she doesn't care as long as there are words in it, maybe she has some sort of clear standard.

Apparently quite smart, she's among the top in our year.

Whenever test results are posted, Hitagi Senjogahara's name is one of the first ten on the list. Whatever the subject. It's presumptuous of me, who can't pass a non-math test, even to compare myself to her, but our brains must be structured in fundamentally different ways.

She doesn't seem to have any friends.

Not a single one.

I have yet to witness Senjogahara exchanging words with someone—the shrewd take might be that her constant reading is a behavior intended to tell you not to speak to her because she is reading, a way of building walls around herself. In fact, I've sat in the same classroom as her for two years and change, and can state with certainty that I've never spoken a word to her in that time. I can and do. Senjogahara's voice is synonymous, for me, with the reedy "I don't know" that she utters like a catchphrase whenever a teacher calls on her in class (whether or not it's a question she clearly knows the answer to, she only ever replies, "I don't know"). Schools are strange places where people without friends routinely form a sort of community (or a colony) of people without friends (myself included, until last year), but Senjogahara seems to be exempt from this rule too. Of course, it's not like she's getting bullied, either. She isn't being persecuted or avoided in any deep, or light, way as far as I can tell. Like that's her natural place to be, with a cool face, Senjogahara goes on reading in one corner of the classroom. She goes on building walls around herself.

Like it's natural for her to be there.

Like it's natural not to be here.

Not that it's any big deal. At our three-year high school, with two hundred students in each grade, you end up sharing a living space with about a thousand people in all during your stay if you include the graduating and incoming classes and the faculty. Start wondering how many of those people mean anything to you, and the answer is going to be bleak for just about anyone.

Even if I meet the odd fortune of sharing a class with someone for three years, and still don't exchange a single word with that person, I don't find it sad. I'd simply look back on it someday and think: Oh, yes, I guess that's how things were. I have no idea what I'll be doing a year down the line, after graduating from high school, but I certainly wouldn't be conjuring up Senjogahara's face—I probably wouldn't be able to.

And that's fine. Senjogahara must be fine with that, too. Not just her, but everyone at my school has to be fine with it. Actually, it's feeling gloomy about the matter that's fundamentally misguided.

That's what I thought.

But.

One such day.

To be precise, the eighth of May, after my hellish joke of a spring break came to an end, I became a third year, and my nightmarish fantasy of a Golden Week wrapped up.

I was dashing up the school stairs, latish as usual, and just reached a landing, when a girl came falling down from the sky.

That girl was Hitagi Senjogahara.

Again, to be precise, she wasn't so much falling down from the sky as simply falling backwards after having missed a step—and I'm sure I could've dodged her, but instead I reflexively caught Senjogahara's body.

It was probably the right decision over dodging her.

No, maybe it was the wrong one.

Why?

Because Senjogahara's body, which I reflexively caught, was so— incredibly light. Unfunnily, bizarrely, eerily light.

As if she wasn't here.

That's right.

Senjogahara weighed so little that she nearly didn't at all.

0 0 2

"Senjogahara?"

Hanekawa tilted her head in response to my question. "Is something the matter with Senjogahara?"

"Nothing like that…" I answered vaguely. "I was just kind of wondering about her."

"Huh."

"I mean, you know, isn't that a weird and interesting name? Hitagi Senjogahara?"

"…You do realize that Senjogahara is the name of a place."

"Er, no, not that part. I was talking about, um, her given name."

"Senjogahara's? You mean Hitagi? Is it that strange? I want to say it's a term related to construction."

"You know everything, don't you?"

"Not everything. I just know what I know." While Hanekawa didn't seem fully satisfied with my explanation, instead of pressing me any further, she said, "You're interested in someone other than yourself, Araragi? That's unusual."

Mind your own business, I told her.

Tsubasa Hanekawa.

The president of our class.

More than that, she's a girl who embodies what a class president should be. Her prim and proper braids, her glasses, her good manners and good behavior, how incredibly serious and loved by the teachers she is, puts her on the endangered species list in this day and age even if you count manga and anime. The way she holds herself makes you wonder if she's been a class president her entire life and is going to be one in some capacity even after graduating. In other words, a class president among class presidents. Possibly a class president chosen by the gods, as one person has been rumoring like it's the unvarnished truth (that would be me).

We were in different classes our first and second years, but for our third year, we were placed together. Though I had heard of her before that, of course I had. If Senjogahara's grades are among the top in our year, Tsubasa Hanekawa's are at the very top. She regularly pulls off unbelievable stunts like scoring a perfect 600 across six courses in five core subjects, and yes, I still remember her utterly monstrous results for the first semester finals our second year like it was yesterday, when across every single subject, including P.E. and Art, she missed only one question, a Japanese History fill-in-the-blank. You hear about celebrities like that whether you want to or not.

And.

The nastiest part—okay, I know it's a good thing, but either way, most annoyingly, Hanekawa is a very caring and decent person. What is actually nasty about her is that she's very single-minded. As is often the case with too-serious people, once she decides on something, no lever will ever budge her. I already had a brief encounter with Hanekawa during spring break, and afterwards, as soon as our new classes were announced and we found out we'd be together, she declared to me, "I'm gonna make sure you turn your life around."

I'm no juvenile delinquent, nor really a problem child. I was a mere class ornament, according to my own assessment, so her proclamation struck me like a bolt from the blue. But no amount of convincing could halt her single-minded delusion, and before I knew it, I was appointed class vice president, which is why, at that moment, after school on the eighth of May, I was still in my classroom alone with Hanekawa hashing out what to do for the mid-June culture festival.

"Culture festival or not, we're third-years now," Hanekawa said. "We

won't be doing much. Studying for college exams is more important."
Prioritizing exam prep over the culture festival, without batting an eye, indeed made her a class president among class presidents. "With a vague survey, the suggestions would be all over the board and just a waste of time. We could go ahead and narrow down the options between us and have everyone vote on those. Are you good with that?"

"Why not? It has a nice democratic veneer."

"You always make things sound so awful, Araragi. Such cynicism."

"That's not cynicism. Hey, you're making me feel like a cartoon sidekick. Tongari, to be exact."

"For reference, Araragi, what did your class do for the culture festival last year and the year before?"

"A haunted house and a cafe."

"How standard. Too standard. You could go so far as to say commonplace."

"I guess."

"You could go so far as to say vulgar."

"Don't go that far."

"Ahaha," she laughed.

"And anyway, wouldn't it be a good idea to do something commonplace this time around? It's not all about our visitors, we need to enjoy our day, too… Oh. Come to think of it—Senjogahara didn't participate in the culture festival either."

Neither last year, nor the year before.

Well, it isn't just the culture festival. Anything you could call an event, anything other than regular classes, Senjogahara basically skips. Sports day, of course, but also school trips, field trips, educational visits, the whole bunch of them. Her doctor forbids her from partaking in any strenuous activity—or something. It seemed strange now that I thought about it. Strenuous exercise, I could understand, but the weird nuance of "strenuous activity"—

But if—

If *that* wasn't some illusion on my part.

If Senjogahara does not weigh *anything*.

That ban would definitely apply to any activity at all outside of the classroom, including P.E., where she was liable to come in contact with a large, unspecified number of people.

"Are you that interested in Senjogahara?" Hanekawa asked.

"Not really, but—"

"Well, boys do like girls who're prone to illness. Ugh, yuck. Filthy, filthy," she teased me. She sounded more sincere than usual, though.

"Prone to illness, huh?"

Sure, she was prone to it.

But was that really an illness?

Was illness it?

Her body being weak, and her being light as a result, made sense—but *that* went beyond such an explanation.

Thin girl or not, a human being had fallen from close to the top of the stairs to the landing. Normally, it was a situation where even the person catching her could get hurt pretty badly.

And yet—there had been barely any impact.

"But don't you know Senjogahara better than I do, Araragi? Why ask me? I mean, you've been in the same class three years in a row, haven't you?"

"If you put it that way, yes—but I thought a girl might know another girl's circumstances a bit better."

"Circumstances…" Hanekawa chuckled drily. "If a girl had any, wouldn't that be the last thing I should go around telling a boy?"

"True," I said. Of course it was. "So, um, think of this as the class vice president asking the class president a question, as the class vice president. What kind of person is Senjogahara?"

"So that's your move."

Hanekawa stopped scribbling out the list she had been making as we conversed (endlessly jotting down and erasing candidates since "haunted house" and "cafe") and crossed her arms in thought. "Because her family name means 'battlefield,' it might make her seem fraught with danger at first, but she's actually a problem-free model student. She's smart, and she takes, say, her cleaning duty seriously."

"I'm sure. Even I can tell that much. I want to know something I can't figure out on my own."

"But we've only been in the same class for about a month. I guess I really don't know her. We had Golden Week off in there, too."

"Yeah, Golden Week."

"Hm? Did something happen then?"

"Nope. Keep going."

"Ah…all right. Senjogahara doesn't talk much—and it seems like she doesn't have any friends. I've tried talking to her a number of times, but it's like she's put up these walls around her."

"………"

What could I say, Hanekawa lived up to her caring reputation. Of course, that was why I was asking her.

"It's—a tough case," she said. In a grave tone. "Maybe it's because of her illness. She was so much more cheerful and energetic in middle school."

"In middle school? Wait, Hanekawa, you and Senjogahara went to the same middle school?"

"What? Isn't that why you're asking me?" Hanekawa made a face like she was the one who never saw it coming. "Yes, we're from the same middle school. Kiyokaze Public Middle School. We used to be in different classes back then, too, but—Senjogahara was famous."

More famous than you? I almost said that, but I caught myself in time. Hanekawa hated being treated as famous more than anything. Personally, I thought she needed to be more self-aware, but she seemed to think of herself as "a regular girl who had nothing to recommend her but being on the serious side." She wholeheartedly bought the cant that anyone who tried hard enough did well in school.

"She was pretty, and she was a good athlete, too," Hanekawa said.

"An athlete…"

"She was the star of the track team. Some of her records should still be standing."

"The track team, huh?"

In other words.

She wasn't *like that* in middle school. Cheerful and energetic—two more qualities I couldn't imagine from the Senjogahara I knew, to be honest.

"So I did hear a lot about her," Hanekawa told me.

"Like what?"

"How nice and sociable she is. How kind she is to everyone alike, all this almost excessive talk about her being a good, hardworking person. Like how her father is some big shot at a foreign-owned company, but her not being stuck-up one bit despite living in an amazing mansion and being amazingly rich. How despite her greatness, she still reaches for greater heights."

"She sounds like some kind of superwoman."

Those stories must have been only half-serious.

Rumors are rumors.

"That was all back then, of course," Hanekawa noted.

"…Back then."

"I did hear after starting high school that she'd fallen ill—still, to be frank, when we became classmates this year I was shocked. She wasn't someone who would sit in the corner of the classroom like that, even by accident."

Though it had been just my image of her, Hanekawa added.

It certainly had been just her image.

People change.

Your middle school days and high school life are worlds apart. That went for me, and for Hanekawa, too. It had to be the same for Senjogahara. She must have gone through a lot, and maybe it was true that she was simply ill. Maybe she'd lost her radiant personality for no other reason. Maybe she'd lost a lot of her fill of cheer. When your body weakened, your spirit tended to sag too, especially if you used to be active. So Hanekawa's speculation was probably on the mark.

If not for that morning.

"But—and I probably shouldn't be saying this—Senjogahara…" resumed Hanekawa.

"What?"

"Compared to then, she's so much prettier now."

"………"

"Her presence is so—evanescent."

The words were enough to silence me.

That…

Evanescent presence.

As if—she had none.

Like a ghost?

Hitagi Senjogahara.

The girl who is always ill.

She—with no weight.

Rumors are—rumors.

Urban legends.

Street gossip.

Tall tales.

Only half-serious, as it were.

"Oh, yeah. I just remembered," I said.

"Hm?"

"Oshino wanted to talk to me."

"Mister Oshino? Why?"

"Well—to help with his work."

"O…kay?" Hanekawa reacted uncertainly.

She seemed suspicious at my sudden change of topic—or rather, blatant curtailment of it. My uncertain phrasing, "to help with his work," could only have deepened her suspicion. This, I thought, is why I don't like dealing with smart people.

Couldn't she just play along?

Standing up from my chair, I continued a bit forcedly, "So me, I need to leave. Can you take care of the rest, Hanekawa?"

"You can for today if you promise to make up for it. There isn't any important work left, so I'll let you go this time. We wouldn't want to keep Mister Oshino waiting," Hanekawa was kind enough to say anyway.

Oshino's name seemed to have worked on her. He had saved her ass, just as he had saved mine, so being ungrateful must have been out of the question. Well, naturally, I'd taken that into account, but it wasn't a complete lie.

"Then can I pick all of the options for our activity? I'll have you confirm them later, though."

"Yeah, I'll let you handle it," I said.

"Send my regards to Mister Oshino."

"I will."

With that, I stepped out of the classroom.

003

Exiting the classroom and closing the door behind me, I took a step forward, when I heard a voice at my back.

"What were you discussing with Hanekawa?"

I turned to face it.

As I did, I had yet to grasp who it was—the voice was unfamiliar. But I'd heard it somewhere before. Yes, that reedy "I don't know" that she uttered like some catchphrase whenever a teacher called on her during class—

"Don't move."

With her second line, I realized that I was dealing with Senjogahara. I also realized that the moment I turned, Senjogahara, as if aiming through a narrow gap, had stuck a box cutter, blade amply extended, right into my oral cavity.

The blade of a box cutter.

Pressed snugly against the inside of my left cheek.

"…ck!"

"Actually, no. I should have said, 'You can move, but it would be very risky.'"

Neither held back, nor in a rough manner, but with just the right amount of strength—the blade stretched the flesh of my cheek.

All I could do was open my mouth wide like an idiot and unflinchingly follow Senjogahara's warning—and stand there immobile.

Scary, I thought.

Not about the box cutter's blade.

Hitagi Senjogahara, who could do such a thing and glare at me with perfectly unwavering, shudderingly cold eyes—was scary.

So she—

She was someone with such a hazardous gaze.

I was convinced.

Seeing that gaze of hers, I was convinced that the edge of the box cutter nestled inside my left cheek was neither dull from use, nor by any means the spine.

"Curiosity is such a cockroach, isn't it? Flocking to precisely the secrets that people want untouched. How insufferable. You dare get on my nerves, the trifling insect that you are."

"H-Hey..."

"What's the matter? Is the right side feeling lonely? Why didn't you say so?"

Instead of her right hand which held the box cutter, her left hand rose. It moved so fast I half-expected a slap and braced myself *against gritting my teeth*, but I was wrong. That wasn't it.

Senjogahara held a stapler in her left hand.

Before I could make it out clearly, she inserted it into my mouth. Not the entire thing, of course, which would have been preferable— Senjogahara had inserted it as if to clamp my right cheek, ready to staple.

Then, gently—it clamped.

As though to staple.

"K...ha..."

It was the larger side loaded with staples that had been stuck in. My mouth was now a standing-room-only affair, and naturally I couldn't form any words. With just the box cutter, while moving was out, I might have been able to talk—but I didn't even want to try now. I didn't want to think about it.

Inserting a thin and sharp box cutter first to make me open my mouth wide, then immediately following up with a stapler—it was a meticulously planned and dreadfully well-executed feat.

The last time various things had been thrust in my mouth was in seventh grade when I had a cavity on an adult tooth treated, dammit! Ever since, I've brushed after every breakfast, lunch, and dinner and chewed xylitol gum tirelessly, just so I'd never have to go through that again, but look where I was.

Talk about the rug getting pulled out from under me.

I blink my eyes—and this happens.

It was difficult to believe that Hanekawa was picking out candidates for the culture festival on the other side of a measly wall when an otherwise nondescript private school hallway formed such a bizarre space.

Hanekawa…

Senjogahara's family name "might make her seem fraught with danger at first"? She lived up to her name perfectly…

Hanekawa was a worse judge of character than I thought!

"Now that you asked Hanekawa about what I was like in middle school, who's next? Our teacher, Hoshina? Or would you like to cut straight to the chase and go to our health teacher, Harukami?"

"………"

I couldn't speak.

However she took that, Senjogahara let out a huge exasperated sigh. "I can't believe how careless I was. I try to be twice as careful as the average person when I climb stairs, but where did that get me? They're not kidding when they say a single fart can ruin a hundred days of sermons."

"………"

Even though I was in a fix, hearing a fair teenaged maiden utter the word "fart" felt wrong to me. Maybe I'm a sweet guy after all.

"An actual banana peel on the floor right then and there. Who would have imagined?"

"………"

My life was now in the hands of a girl who had slipped on a banana peel.

Wait, why was it even lying on a school staircase?

"You've noticed, haven't you," Senjogahara asked me.

Her gaze was still hazardous.

A cloistered princess? Yeah, right.

"That's right—I don't weigh a thing."

She weighed nothing.

"Well, it's not as if I don't at all—a girl my height and body type would have an average body weight in the high forties, in kilograms—"

So fifty kilograms.

My left cheek was pushed outward, and my right cheek was compressed.

"……gh!"

"No funny thoughts. You were imagining me in the nude just now, weren't you?"

That was completely off the mark, but she was sure sharp.

"An average body weight in the high forties, in kilograms," Senjogahara insisted.

She wasn't going to budge on that one.

"But my actual body weight is five kilograms."

Five kilograms.

Not much more than a newborn baby.

If you think of a dozen-pound dumbbell, that number isn't quite close to zero, but considering that the mass is distributed across the size of an entire person, in terms of density—of how it realistically feels, it was as good as having no weight.

Catching her would be a piece of cake.

"Now, if you want to be completely accurate, it's only that a scale displays my weight as five kilos—I personally don't notice it. Nothing has changed for me from my high-forties days."

Did that mean…

Gravity affected her less than a normal person? Not just mass, but volume—if I remembered correctly, the specific gravity of water is 1, and since the human body consists mostly of water, its specific gravity and density is also about 1—in which case, simply put, Senjogahara was only a tenth as dense.

If that was her bone density, she'd get osteoporosis in no time at all. Her heart and her brain wouldn't function correctly either.

So it couldn't have been that.

A question of numbers, it wasn't.

"I know what you're thinking," she said.

"……"

"Staring at my breasts like that. Disgusting."

"……ck!"

I wasn't thinking about that, I promise!

It seemed that Senjogahara was a pretty self-conscious high school girl. Who could blame her, with how pretty she looked? I wished the class president working a wall away from us would take a cue.

"This is why I can't stand superficial people."

Clearing up that misunderstanding seemed impossible at the moment—in any case, what I was thinking was that far from being always ill, Senjogahara found herself in a body that completely belied the package description. Weighing five kilos should have made her more than ill, and downright feeble, but not here. On the contrary, if I may, she was like an alien who had come to Earth from a star with ten times the gravity. You'd expect her to have excellent athletic skills, especially if she used to be on the track team. Sure, collisions weren't her strong suit, but…

"It happened after I graduated middle school and before I came to this high school," Senjogahara said. "During that fuzzy, in-between period when you're neither a middle schooler nor a high schooler, nor even on spring recess—I turned into *this*."

"……"

"*It happened after—I met a crab.*"

C-Crab?

Did she just say "a crab"?

A crab, like the ones you eat in the winter?

Those arthropods, classified under Crustacea Decapoda?

"It took my weight away—all of it."

"……"

"It's fine, you don't have to understand. I'm only telling you this because it'd be a huge annoyance if you kept sniffing around. Araragi—listen, Koyomi Araragi."

Senjogahara spoke my name, and repeated it.

"I weigh nothing—I have no weight. Nothing at all you could

call weight. What a fiasco. It's like I'm a character from a supernatural manga series. Do you like Yosuke Takahashi?"

"......"

"The only person at school who knows about this is our health teacher, Harukami. Just our health teacher Harukami, so far. Not Principal Yoshiki, not Vice Principal Shima, not Irinaka in charge of our year, not Hoshina, our homeroom teacher. Only Harukami—and you, Araragi."

"......"

"So, what should I do to make you keep my secret to yourself? What should I do, for my own sake? What kind of deal are we going to have to *cut* to *staple* your mouth shut?"

A box cutter.

A stapler.

Was she in her right mind? What a way to corner a classmate. Did she still call herself a human being? Knowing that I'd sat in the same room with such a terrifying person for over two years sent a real shiver down my spine.

"The doctor at the hospital says that the cause is unknown—or rather, that there might not be a cause. Such a lame conclusion to come to after fiddling around for ages with a stranger's body in humiliating ways. You know what he said? 'It is as it was, as it is now.' How ridiculous," Senjogahara said, self-mockingly. "Until middle school, I was a normal, cute girl."

"........."

Putting aside for now the fact that she called herself cute.

It was true that she made regular visits to the hospital.

Arriving late, leaving early, simply not showing up.

And—the health teacher.

I tried putting myself in Senjogahara's shoes.

Unlike me, who *just coped with it for two brief weeks over spring break*, ever since she entered high school, it *had stayed that way*.

What did she resign herself to?

What did she give up on?

She'd had more than enough time to do so.

"Are you feeling sorry for me? Oh, how generous of you," Senjogahara spat as if she'd read my mind. Disgusting, I could all but hear her add. "But it's not generosity that I want."

"……"

"I want your silence and your indifference, nothing more. If you have those, could you give them to me? You value your cheeks, as free of pimples as they are, don't you?"

And then.

Senjogahara smiled.

"If you promise me your silence and your indifference, Araragi, then nod twice. I'll consider any other action, even freezing, as hostile behavior and promptly move to attack."

There wasn't a shred of reluctance in her words.

Having no choice, I nodded.

I nodded to her twice.

"There."

Upon seeing this—Senjogahara seemed to relax.

Despite the fact that I had no choice, that it was neither a transaction nor an agreement and I could only consent to her demand, she seemed to relax when I went ahead and complied.

"Thank you," she said.

Then she detached the box cutter from the inside of my left cheek and withdrew it slowly, more languidly than cautiously. I did sense from the movement of her hand that she was taking care not to scar me inside my mouth by mistake.

She retracted the box cutter's blade.

Click-click-click-click.

Next, the stapler.

"…Ngeek?!"

Ka-chunk.

I couldn't believe it.

The stapler—had clamped down hard. Then, before I could react to the immense pain, she handily popped it out of my mouth.

I crumpled into a ball on the spot.

Cradling my cheek, from outside.

"Gh...urrk..."

"You're not going to scream? Impressive," Senjogahara said above me, as if she hadn't done a thing.

Looking down on me.

"I'll let you off at that for today. I hate being so lenient, but you did promise, so I ought to show you some good will."

"...Y-You—"

Ka-chunk.

As if to talk over me, Senjogahara made an overlapping sound with the stapler, clamping it in the air.

A deformed staple fell before my eyes.

I couldn't help but flinch.

A reflex, if you will.

I'd been classically conditioned in a single go.

"Okay, Araragi. Be sure to ignore me starting tomorrow. Fare thee well!"

With that, uninterested in my response, Senjogahara turned her heels and began walking down the hall. Before I could even get up from my balled position, she turned a corner and vanished from sight.

"Sh-She's like some devil."

Our brains were structured in—fundamentally different ways.

Despite the situation and despite her words, some part of me had assumed that she wouldn't really. In which case, maybe I should be blessing my good fortune that she had chosen the stapler and not the box cutter.

I gently brushed my cheek again, not to ease the pain this time, but to check on it.

"........."

Good.

I was okay, it hadn't punched through.

Next, I stuck my own finger in my mouth. Using my left hand, since this was my right cheek. It didn't take long to come upon what I was looking for.

Although I could guess from the sharp pain, which neither vanished nor receded, this did away with my peaceful line of thinking that maybe the first staple actually hadn't been loaded, that it had been no more than a threat designed to threaten... To be honest, I'd gotten my hopes up for that one.

But it was fine.

If the staple hadn't punched through, that meant it was not overly deformed...and close to its original shape, a rectangle with a missing side. It wasn't hooked in, so to speak, which meant I'd be able to rip it out without meeting too much resistance.

I pinched it between my thumb and index finger, and yanked.

The sharp pain was joined by a dull, metallic taste.

I seemed to be spurting blood.

"Kh...ahh..."

I was fine.

This much—I could take fine.

Licking the two puncture wounds that had formed on the inside of my cheek, I bent the staple I'd taken out and placed it in the pocket of my school-issued jacket. I also picked up the staple Senjogahara had dropped and did the same. It'd be dangerous if someone stepped on it with bare feet. Staples looked like magnum ammo to me now.

"Hm? You're still here, Araragi?"

As I was doing this, Hanekawa emerged from the classroom.

She seemed to be done.

Why couldn't she have come sooner?

Or maybe her timing was right.

"Don't you need to hurry to Mister Oshino's?" Hanekawa asked suspiciously.

She hadn't noticed a thing, it seemed.

Just a wall in between—right, she'd been beyond a mere, thin wall. Hitagi Senjogahara, who nevertheless pulled off an act of derring-do without Hanekawa noticing a thing—was indeed someone to be reckoned with.

"Hey, Hanekawa... Do you like bananas?"

"Hm? Uh, I don't particularly dislike them. They're nutritious, too, so if I had to choose between like and dislike, then sure, I like them."

"Even if you love them, don't ever have them at school!"

"E-Excuse me?"

"Just eating them wouldn't be all that terrible, but if I ever catch you tossing a leftover peel on the stairs, I'll never forgive you!"

"What are you talking about, Araragi?!" Hanekawa said with a puzzled expression and a hand to her mouth.

Of course she did.

"Anyway, Araragi, what about Mister—"

"I'm going to Oshino's—as we speak."

With that, I rushed off, blowing past Hanekawa. "Yikes! Hey, Araragi, don't run in the halls! Don't make me tell on you!" her voice came from behind, but naturally I ignored it.

I ran.

I just ran.

I turned the corner to reach the stairs.

I was on the fourth floor.

She couldn't have gone that far yet.

With a hop, step, and a jump, I skipped two, three, then four stairs at a time—and arrived on the landing.

I could feel the impact in my legs.

An impact commensurate to my weight.

Then this impact, too—

Senjogahara had to be lacking.

She weighed nothing.

She had no weight.

Which meant—her footing wasn't secure.

A crab.

A crab, she'd said.

"Not this way—this way."

She couldn't have gone off sideways at that point. Never thinking that I'd come chasing after her, she would have proceeded straight ahead, toward the school gates. She had to be a member of the no-extracurriculars club, but even if she were affiliated with an actual something-or-other, no activity would kick off at such a late hour. With that assumption, I descended the stairs from the third floor to the second, not hesitating for a moment. I leapt down them.

Then from the second floor to the landing of the first.

Senjogahara was there.

I was practically rolling down the stairs in pursuit and creating a ruckus, so she must have caught on, because she still had her back to me but had already turned her head.

With a cold look.

"...I can't believe you," she said. "Or rather, I'm honestly surprised. As far as I can remember, being able to feel rebellious so soon after having that much done to you is a first, Araragi."

"A first..."

She'd done it to others, too?

What was that about "a hundred days of sermons," then?

Come to think of it, though, it made sense that keeping a secret like "not having any weight," which the slightest contact could divulge, was impossible realistically speaking...

And she'd said "so far," hadn't she?

Maybe she really was some devil.

"Also," she added, "pain in your oral cavity shouldn't be so easy to recover from. Normally, you can't budge from the spot for a good ten minutes."

She was speaking from experience.

Too scary.

"All right, I get it. I get it, Araragi. Your 'eye for an eye' attitude agrees with my own sense of justice. If you're down for it..."

Senjogahara fanned her arms out to both sides as she spoke.

"Let's have ourselves a war."

In her hands were—stationery tools of every kind, the box cutter, the stapler, and more: sharpened HB pencil, compass, tricolor ballpoint pen, mechanical pencil, super glue, rubber band, paper clip, bulldog clip, power clipper, permanent marker, safety pin, fountain pen, correction fluid, scissors, cellophane tape, sewing kit, letter opener, plastic isosceles triangle, thirty-centimeter ruler, protractor, rubber cement, an assortment of chisels, paint, paperweight, ink.

......

I began to feel that some day in the future, I'd be groundlessly persecuted by society for the mere act of having shared a class with her.

I personally saw the super glue as the most dangerous.

"W-Wait, wait, no. We're not having a war," I said.

"We're not? Oh, well."

She sounded a bit disappointed.

But her arms were still outstretched.

Her deadly weapons, otherwise known as stationery, still gleamed.

"Then what do you want?"

"I was thinking, just maybe," I replied, "I might be able to help you out."

"Help me out?"

From the bottom of her heart, it seemed—

She sneered like I was a fool.

No, maybe she was angry.

"Give me a break. Didn't I tell you I don't need any cheap sympathy? You can't do a thing for me. Keep mum and pay no attention to me, that's all I want."

"……"

"Generosity, too—I will deem as hostile behavior."

With those words, she climbed one step.

She had to be serious.

Our earlier interaction had taught me all too well that she wasn't the hesitant type. Damn well.

And that's why.

That's why, without saying a word, I stuck a finger against the edge of my lips and tugged to show her my cheek.

My right cheek, with my right hand.

Naturally, this exposed the inside of my mouth.

"Wha-"

The sight couldn't but shock even Senjogahara. The deadly weapons otherwise known as stationery spilled and fell from both of her hands.

"You—how did…"

I could tell even before she'd asked.

Yes.

The taste of blood was already gone.

The wound Senjogahara had dealt to my mouth with her stapler had healed without a trace.

004

It happened during spring break.

I was attacked by a vampire.

In this day and age of real, working maglev trains, where overseas school trips are nothing unusual, it's embarrassing enough to make me want to go into hiding, but regardless, I was attacked by a vampire.

She was blood-chillingly gorgeous.

A beautiful demon.

She was—such a beautiful demon.

Though they're concealed behind the collar of my uniform's jacket, the traces of her deep bite still remain on my neck. I'm hoping that my hair will grow out before it gets hot out, but putting that aside— usually, when regular people get attacked by a vampire, the story goes that they're saved by an expert vampire hunter, by Christianity's special forces, or perhaps even by a vampire-slaying vampire who hunts its own kind, but in my case, I was saved by a shabby old dude who happened to be passing by.

Thanks to him, I was somehow able to *turn back into a human*—fine again with sunlight, crosses, garlic, and such, but the effect, or rather, the aftereffect the experience had on me was a remarkable improvement in my physical abilities. Not my athletic abilities, mind you, but like my metabolism, in the way of recuperating. While I don't know how I would've ended up if the box cutter had ripped my cheek apart, it takes less than thirty seconds to heal something like a simple staple stabbed through my flesh. At any rate, to begin with, wounds in the oral cavity tend to heal quickly for any organism.

"Oshino—a Mister Oshino?"

"Right. Mèmè Oshino."

"Mèmè Oshino, huh—quite an adorable-sounding name, I have to say."

"You shouldn't get your hopes up on that count. He's a weathered, middle-aged, thirty-something."

"I see. But as a kid, he must have been quite a *moé* character."

"Don't look at flesh-and-blood people like that. And wait, do you even know what that word means?"

"It's a part of common learning these days," Senjogahara said blithely. "And you call characters like me *tsundere*, right? Cold and mean at first, but loving once you get to know me?"

"………"

With how cold she was, "tundra" suited her better.

But I digress.

About twenty minutes by bicycle from Naoetsu Private High School, which Hanekawa, Senjogahara, and I attended, stands a cram school slightly separated from any homes.

Stood.

Apparently, a few years ago, it took the full brunt of a big cram school chain setting up shop in front of the station, ran into financial troubles, and went out of business. By the time I learned of the four-story building's existence, though, it was an abandoned ruin through and through, so all this is second-hand info.

Danger.

Private Property.

No Trespassing.

Despite a plethora of such signs and the Safety First fence surrounding it, access is as good as unrestricted thanks to all the gaps.

In these ruins—lives Oshino.

He's taken up residence, without permission.

For an entire month now, starting during spring break.

"God, my bottom hurts. It's numb. And my skirt got wrinkled," Senjogahara said.

"Not my fault."

"Stop trying to talk your way out of this, or I'll lop it off."

"Which body part?!"

"This is my first time riding on a bicycle with someone else. Can't you be a little more generous?"

Wasn't generosity hostile behavior for her?

Everything this girl said and did was beyond the pale.

"So, how exactly might I have tried?" I asked.

"Well, as a small suggestion, couldn't you have given me your bag to use as a cushion?"

"Do you not give a crap about anyone other than yourself?"

"Please, don't use such rude language with me. I said it was only a small suggestion."

How did repeating that make it any better?

It was most questionable.

"You know, I bet even Marie Antoinette was a little more modest and humble than you," I said.

"She's something like my disciple," Senjogahara replied.

"In what timeline?!"

"I wish you'd stop casually riffing off of everything I say. You're acting like we're buddies or something. Listening to you, a stranger might even think that we're classmates."

"We are classmates!"

How much was she going to disavow me?

That was just too cold.

"Jeez..." I lamented. "I guess dealing with you requires an unbelievable amount of patience."

"Araragi. The way you put that, it almost sounds like I'm the one who's hard to get along with, not you."

That's exactly what I wanted to say.

"Actually, where's your own bag?" I asked her. "You're empty-handed. Do you not carry one?" In fact, I couldn't remember ever seeing Senjogahara carrying anything with her.

"I have all my textbooks stored inside my head. So I just leave them in my school locker. If I hide all my stationery around my body, there's no need for a bag. And in my case, gym clothes are out."

"Ah, I see."

"If both of my hands aren't free, it's harder to fight when the time comes."

"……"

Her entire body was a weapon.

She was a human weapon.

"The only issue I have is with hygiene products because it bothers me to keep them at school. With no friends, I can't borrow them from anyone, either."

"…You're being awfully open about this, you know."

"Why not? Menses is Latin for month. It's a natural phenomenon, nothing to be embarrassed of. I'd say it's more indecent to be furtive about it."

I wasn't so sure about not being at least a little furtive.

No, it was a matter of personal choice.

Not my place to say.

Maybe what I ought to be making a note of instead was her even more open admission—that she didn't have any friends.

"Oh, that's right," I said, turning to face her after reaching an "entrance."

Though it was all the same to me, I'd searched for a particularly large one because, to judge from her earlier comment about her skirt, Senjogahara, being a girl after all, might not want her uniform to fray.

"Let me hold on to your stationery or whatever."

"Huh?"

"Take it out. I'll hold on to it."

"Huh? Huh?"

From her expression, you might think that I'd made an outrageous demand. It seemed to ask if something was wrong with my head.

"Oshino is, well, he's a weird dude, but he did technically save my life—"

Not only that.

He'd saved Hanekawa's, too.

"—and I can't have the man who did face a dangerous person. So I'll hold on to your stationery."

"You only tell me after we've come this far?" Senjogahara glared at me. "It seems I've stepped into a trap."

"……"

Nah, that was way overboard.

But Senjogahara struggled silently with the matter for a while. She scowled at me now and then or stared at a point by her feet.

I wondered if she was going to turn around and leave, but at last, like someone prepared for the worst, she said, "Understood. Take them."

Then, taking out a myriad of stationery from across her body like it was some magic show, she began handing them to me. What I'd seen earlier on the landing was only the tip of her badness and madness. You could've told me her pockets stretched into the fourth dimension; it could've been twenty-second-century science. I'd told her I'd hold on to it, but she was producing so much materiel I was starting to doubt if my bag was up to it.

…Someone like her strolling around in public unrestricted surely amounted to negligence on the part of the authorities…

"Don't get me wrong," Senjogahara warned after she'd finished giving everything to me. "It's not like I'm letting my guard down around you."

"You might as well…"

"If you're trying to get back at me for stabbing you with a staple by tricking me into entering these desolate ruins, you'll be making the wrong party pay."

"…"

No, as far as which party, I would be right on.

"Understand?" she said. "I have five thousand of my rowdiest pals ready to attack your family if they don't hear from me at least once every minute."

"It's fine… Stop worrying."

"You mean you won't even need a whole minute?!"

"I am not that boxer."

And hold on. She didn't think twice about targeting my family.

I couldn't believe her.

On top of that, five thousand pals? What a lie.

A bold lie for someone who had no friends.

"Say, I hear your two little sisters are still in middle school."

"………"

She knew my family's makeup.

She might've lied, but she wasn't joking.

In any case, displaying a modicum of my "immortality" hadn't made her trust me one bit. Oshino always said that relationships of trust were important in these things, and my current situation wasn't a good one from that perspective.

But what can you do.

From here, the problem was Senjogahara's alone.

I was merely a guide.

We passed through a tear in the chain-link fence onto the grounds, and into the building. It was still evening, but it was fairly dark inside. There was a lot of clutter on the floor after days and months of neglect, and you could trip on something if you weren't careful.

That's when I realized.

An empty can lying around was nothing more than an empty can to me, but it had ten times the mass for Senjogahara.

Relatively speaking, that was the case.

It wasn't like in old comics where you spoke of "ten times the gravity" or "a tenth of the gravity" and left it there. The simple take that "lighter equals more athletic" didn't work. Worse, it was this dark, in a place she didn't know. Maybe Senjogahara couldn't be blamed for parading a wild animal's level of caution.

Even if she were ten times faster.

She'd only be a tenth as strong.

Her reluctance to surrender her stationery also began to make sense in that regard.

And—why she didn't carry a bag.

Why she couldn't carry one, either.

"…This way."

Clasping Senjogahara's wrist, I led her forward from the entrance where she'd been standing uncertainly. She was taken aback because I was a bit sudden, but while she gave me a "What?" she followed without resisting.

"Don't expect any thanks," she said.

"I know."

"In fact, you should be thanking me."

"I don't understand?!"

"I put that stapler around your mouth so that it'd hit the inside of your cheek, not the outside. I didn't want to leave a visible wound."

"……"

I couldn't hear that as anything other than an abuser's "It'll show on the face, so punch in the belly" thinking.

"It wouldn't have mattered if it had penetrated," I pointed out.

"I judged that you'd quite likely be fine, going by how thick-skinned your face looks."

"If you're trying to comfort me, it's not working. And 'quite likely'?"

"My intuition is right about a tenth of the time."

"That's all?!"

"Well—" Senjogahara paused before continuing, "it was all wasted consideration in the end."

"…Seems that way."

"If I said that immortality seems convenient, would you feel hurt?" she followed up with a question.

I answered, "Not so much, now."

Not so much—now.

But during spring break?

If someone had said that to me then—the words may have killed me. May have dealt a fatal wound.

"You could say it's convenient—but you could also say it's inconvenient. That's about it."

"How wishy-washy. I don't get it." Senjogahara shrugged. "Is it like when people talk about a 'devil may care' attitude? Satan probably doesn't, but just might?"

"Nothing wishy-washy there. He absolutely doesn't."

"Oh."

"And anyway, I'm not immortal anymore. I just heal a tad faster than normal. Otherwise I'm a regular human."

"Huh, I see," Senjogahara muttered, sounding disappointed. "I was planning on trying all sorts of things on you if I got the chance. Too bad."

"From the sound of it, some very grotesque planning was going on behind my back..."

"How rude. I was only going to &% your /- before *^ing it."

"What do those symbols mean?!"

"And I wanted to do <u>this</u> and <u>that</u> to you, too."

"What is that underlining supposed to suggest?!"

Oshino tended to be on the fourth floor.

The building had an elevator, but it was of course out of service. That meant our options were busting through the elevator's roof and using the cables to climb to the fourth floor, or taking the stairs. I think it'd be fair to say that anyone would pick the latter option.

I started up the stairs, still tugging Senjogahara by the hand.

"Let me tell you one last thing, Araragi."

"What is it?"

"I might not look it with my clothes on, but actually, my body might not be worth breaking the law to make yours."

"......"

It seemed that Miss Hitagi Senjogahara hewed to the highest notions of chastity.

"Was that too roundabout for you? Then let me say it flat-out. If you lay bare your base instincts and rape me, I will do anything and everything in my power to pay you back slash-fiction style."

"......"

As for shame and modesty, she had none at all.

Actually, she was just plain scary.

"You know, this isn't only about what you said just now, but looking at everything you do, Senjogahara, you seem a little, I guess, too self-conscious? Like maybe you should dial down your persecution complex?"

"Ugh. Don't you know that some things are best left unsaid, even if they're true?"

"You were aware of it?!"

"Anyway, this building looks like it's about to collapse. I can't believe this—Oshino person lives here."

"Yeah…well, he's a pretty weird guy."

Though if you asked me how he compared to Senjogahara, at that point I'd have had to think it over.

"Shouldn't we have contacted him in advance?" she fretted. "It's a little late now, but we're the ones who're seeking advice…"

"Putting aside my shock at your apparent display of common sense, he unfortunately doesn't carry a cell phone."

"How enigmatic. Almost a suspicious character. What exactly does he do?"

"I don't know the details, but—he says he *specializes* in cases like mine and yours."

"Hmph."

It was far from a proper explanation, but Senjogahara didn't try to dig any deeper. Perhaps she thought that she was about to meet him anyway, or that there was no point in asking. She was right either way.

"Hey. You wear your watch on your right arm, Araragi."

"Huh? Oh, yeah."

"Are you a contrarian or something?"

"Start by asking if I'm left-handed!"

"Uh huh. Well, are you?"

"……"

I was a contrarian.

The fourth floor.

As the building was originally a cram school, it had three class-like rooms—but with the doors to all three broken, they and the hallway connecting them were now a single area. When I peeked inside the closest one first, wondering where Oshino was:

"Oh, Araragi. So you finally came."

Mèmè Oshino was right there.

Sitting cross-legged atop his makeshift bed (if you could call it that) of a number of rotting desks pushed together and bound with plastic string, he was facing me.

As if he'd been expecting me.

Like always—like he saw it all coming.

As for Senjogahara—she was visibly creeped out.

While I did tell her in advance, Oshino's filthy demeanor significantly deviated, no doubt, from a modern-day high school girl's aesthetic standards. Anyone would look as ragged as him living in these ruins, but even I, a boy, could say that Oshino's appearance was not a hygienic one. If we're to be entirely honest. But most of all, his psychedelic Hawaiian shirt was the fatal blow.

I think this every time I see him, but really, the fact that such a person is my savior can be a downer... Though I'm sure someone as mature as Hanekawa isn't bothered one bit.

"Oh, so you've brought yet another girl with you today, Araragi? You're with a new one every time we meet. Why, I'm quite glad for you."

"Stop making me out to be some sort of sleazebag."

"Hah—hm?"

Oshino cast a distant gaze in Senjogahara's direction.

As if he was looking at something behind her.

"...Nice to meet you, missy. I'm Oshino."

"Nice to meet you—I'm Hitagi Senjogahara."

She'd managed to give him a proper greeting.

So she was discriminating with her acid tongue. At least, it looked like she could be polite to her elders.

"Araragi is my classmate, and he told me about you."

"Huh. Is that so."

Oshino nodded meaningfully.

He looked down, pulled out a cigarette, and put it in his mouth. But instead of lighting it, he kept it there and used it to indicate the windows, or rather, the scenery beyond the random fragments of glass that had long ceased to function as windows.

Then, after waiting for more than long enough, he turned to me.

"So, Araragi. You got a thing for girls with straight bangs?"

"What was it I just told you not to do? And girls with straight bangs? Isn't that what you'd call a plain-old pedophile? Don't lump me in with your generation who had *Full House* airing on TV when you were going through puberty."

"Right." Oshino laughed.

Senjogahara scowled in response.

The word "pedophile" might've been what did it.

"Um—anyway," I said, "get the details from her directly, but Oshino—about two years ago, this girl over here—"

"Don't call me that," Senjogahara commanded me.

"Then what do you want me to call you?"

"Miss Senjogahara."

"……"

Was she in her right mind?

"…Miss-Sen-Joe-Guh-Hara."

"I won't have you saying it like a machine. Say it normally."

"Missy Senjogahara."

She poked me in the eyes.

"You nearly blinded me!"

"An eye for an eye," she said.

"How do you get an eye out of hurt feelings? Where's the equivalence in that?!"

"My inappropriate remarks are an alloy of 40 grams copper, 25 grams zinc, 15 grams nickel, 5 grams bashfulness, and 97 kilograms malice."

"That's almost all malice!"

"Also, I was lying about the bashfulness."

"And now you got rid of the saving grace!"

"Oh, be quiet. I'm going to nickname you 'menstrual cramps' if you don't knock it off."

"That's the kind of bullying people kill themselves over!"

"What do you mean? It's literally a natural phenomenon, nothing to be embarrassed of."

"Then don't be malicious about it!"

Senjogahara seemed to have gotten her fill and finally turned back to Oshino. "Now, before we proceed, allow me one question."

Her tone suggested that she wasn't asking just Oshino, but both me and him, as she pointed to a corner of the classroom. There, holding her knees, crouched a little girl who seemed out of place even in a cram school because she was too little at about eight years old, a pale, blonde girl who wore a helmet and goggles.

"What, exactly, is that child?"

Judging by her phrasing, she recognized that the girl wasn't fully a who. In fact, a prickly glare that surpassed even Senjogahara's and that focused on a single point, Oshino, and didn't waver would have tipped off anyone attuned to such things.

"Oh, you don't have to worry about that," I explained to her before Oshino got a chance. "It's not like she can do anything, she just sits there—it's nothing. A kid who's neither a shadow nor a trace. Not even a name or a presence."

"Hold on a sec, Araragi," Oshino cut in. "You're right to say that she has no shadow, trace, or even a presence, but I gave her a name yesterday. She worked hard over Golden Week, plus it's a huge pain to have nothing to call her by. And without a name, she'll never stop being heinous."

"A name, huh? What is it?" I knew I was abandoning Senjogahara with the question, but I was interested so I asked.

"I named her Shinobu Oshino."

"Shinobu—huh."

A decisively Japanese name. It was also an alternative reading for the "Oshi" in Oshino.

Not that it mattered.

"Written with the character for 'heart' under the one for 'blade.' A fitting name for her, don't you think? I let her reuse my last name as-is, which by luck uses the same character. Double it up for triple the meaning. I'm pretty impressed with my sensibility, if I do say so myself."

"Well, why not."

It really didn't matter.

"After giving it some thought," my savior continued, "it came down to Shinobu Oshino or Oshino Oshino, with an Edo period-style 'o' in the given name, but I decided to prioritize how it sounds over linguistic uniformity. I'm also a fan of the way it resembles missy class president on paper, with two characters for the last name but just one for the first."

"Why not."

It absolutely didn't matter.

Though, well, "Oshino Oshino" did seem out of the question.

"So," Senjogahara said, as if her patience had run out long ago, "what is that child?"

"Like I said—it's nothing," I told her.

A husk of a vampire.

The dregs of a beautiful demon.

You might say so, but what else could I have done? This had nothing to do with Senjogahara anyway. It was my problem. Just my karma, which I merely ought to face for the rest of my life.

"It's nothing? Okay, then."

"……"

What an indifferent woman.

"It's like my grandmother on my father's side always said," she added. "The opposite of hate is not love, but indifference."

"Hold on, what?"

That was somehow so messed up.

Where did that one come from, the bath-pissed church?

"But anyway." Hitagi Senjogahara shifted her gaze from the pale, blonde former vampire, now known as Shinobu Oshino, to Mèmè Oshino. "I heard that you would save me."

"Save you? Now that I can't do," Oshino said in his usual teasing tone. "You're just going to get saved on your own, missy."

"……"

Whoa.

Senjogahara's eyes narrowed by half.

She was manifestly doubtful.

"So far," she said, "five people have spouted similar lines to me. All of them were frauds. Are you one as well, Mister Oshino?"

"Ha hah. You're a spirited one, missy. Something good happen to you?"

Why do you keep provoking her right back, I wondered. It worked on some people, like Hanekawa, but Senjogahara was the last person to try it on.

She was the type to respond to provocation with a preemptive strike.

"N-Now, now," I was forced to step in and mediate.

As if to wedge myself in between the two.

"Keep your nose out of this. I'll kill you."

"……"

So casual a death threat, Senjogahara.

Why should the sparks fall on me?

She was like a firebomb.

She was going to outpace my vocabulary, wasn't she?

"Well, in any case." Oshino's carefree manner offered such a contrast with hers. "We're not going to get anywhere unless you start talking. I'm no good at reading minds. And more importantly, I like dialogue. I'm a talker at heart. But I do keep secrets, so don't you worry."

Senjogahara didn't respond.

"U-Uhm, so to start with a simple explanation—" I began.

"It's fine, Araragi," she interrupted again before I could go over the gist of it. "I'll do it myself."

"Senjogahara—"

"I can do it myself," she said.

005

Two hours later.

I had left the former cram school where Oshino and the vampire now known as Shinobu lived and was at Senjogahara's home.

The Senjogahara residence.

The Tamikura Apartments.

A two-story wooden building built thirty years ago, with a sheet metal communal mailbox out front. It did have a shower and a flush toilet, at least. A so-called one-room apartment measuring barely more than a hundred square feet, with a small sink. Twenty minutes walking to the closest bus stop (not train station, mind you). The rent, including the maintenance fee, neighborhood dues, and utility, estimated at thirty to forty thousand yen a month.

It was very different from what I'd heard from Hanekawa.

It must have shown on my face because Senjogahara explained, "My mother fell for religion, a sketchy one."

Unprompted, like she was making an excuse.

Like she was trying to paper this over.

"She not only gave them everything we owned but took on a huge amount of debt. A believer and her money are soon parted."

"Religion? You mean…"

She was into some money-grubbing cult.

And we all knew what that led to.

"My father took custody of me after my parents filed for an uncontested divorce at the end of last year, and now we live here together. Well, I say that, but I rarely see him because the debts are in his name and he's still working himself to the bone to pay them off. I'm living alone for all intents and purposes and love the freedom."

"……"

"But the school still has my old address on file, so you can't fault Hanekawa for not knowing."

Hey.

Were you allowed to do that?

"I'd rather not announce my whereabouts to people who might become my enemies one day."

"Enemies…"

It sounded overblown, but perhaps such cautiousness wasn't improbable in folks with secrets to keep.

"Senjogahara. When you say your mom fell for religion—could it have been for your sake?"

"What an unpleasant question." Senjogahara laughed. "Who can tell? Beats me. Maybe that wasn't it."

It was—an unpleasant answer.

But perhaps the natural one to an unpleasant question.

My question really had been unpleasant, so much so that I look back and loathe myself for it. I shouldn't have asked, and this was the moment when Senjogahara should have dispensed a lashing with her trusty acid tongue.

Having lived under the same roof, her family couldn't not have noticed that their daughter no longer had any weight—especially her mother. This wasn't school where you could just sit there and take the same classes. An incredible anomaly afflicting the body of their dear only daughter would have come to light right away. Once the doctors had all but thrown in the towel and resorted to an everyday routine of exams, no one could blame you for seeking solace.

Or maybe you weren't free of blame.

I didn't know.

What point was there in acting like I knew?

In any case.

In any case, I was—sitting on a cushion at a low table and staring with glazed eyes at a teacup that had been filled for me in Room 201, Tamikura Apartments, Senjogahara's home.

This was her, so I'd expected to be told, "You wait outside," but she'd invited me right in. She'd even made me tea. It was a bit of a shock.

"I'm going to break your every bone," she said.

"What?"

"I'm sorry. Make yourself at home, I mean."

"………"

"Well, maybe I was right the first time…"

"You nailed it your second try! You couldn't have done better! That's really impressive of you, Senjogahara, not everyone can correct their own mistakes like that!"

…But that was the extent of our conversation, so I was flummoxed. It wasn't like I could utter some naive line about barging into the home of a girl I'd just gotten to know. All I could do was stare at my tea.

Senjogahara was taking a shower right then.

As a rite to cleanse herself, or something.

She was to wash her body with cold water and change into a clean set of clothes, new or old would do—according to Oshino.

Essentially, she had taken me along for this. Well, she almost had to because we'd gone from school to Oshino's place on my bike, and he'd advised as much.

Having glanced around the spartan hundred-odd square feet that looked nothing like a young woman's room, I leaned back on the small clothes drawer behind me—and thought back to what Oshino had said.

"The *omoshi-kani*. A Crab of Weight."

After Senjogahara had conveyed her circumstances—not her life's story exactly, but still, her situation from start to finish—Oshino nodded with an "I see," looked up at the ceiling for a bit, and spoke those words as if they'd just come to him.

"A Crab of Weight?" echoed Senjogahara.

"It's a piece of folklore from the mountainous areas of Kyushu. Depending on the locale, it might be called the weight crab, the heavy crab, the stone-weight crab, or even the *omoishi-gami*. That last instance is playing on *kani*, 'crab,' and *kami*, 'god.' The details vary, but what the stories have in common is people being deprived of *weight*. Encountering it—encountering it in the wrong way apparently makes your presence fade, too."

"Your presence…"

Evanescent.

So—evanescent.

And—so much prettier now.

"Not just your presence," Oshino elaborated. "In some nasty cases, your entire existence. They've got something in the Chubu region called the 'stone-weight stone,' but I think that's something totally different. I mean, that's a stone, and this is a crab."

"A crab? Is it really a crab?"

"Don't be silly, Araragi. They don't catch too many in the mountains of Miyazaki and Oita. We're talking about a legend." Oshino sounded thoroughly appalled. "Sometimes being absent better lends itself to talk. Don't delusions and backbiting tend to get people going?"

"Are crabs Japanese to begin with?"

"Araragi, are you thinking of crawfish? From America? Are you not familiar with Japanese folktales? The Crab and the Monkey. I believe there's a famous crab aberration in Russia, and a good number of them in China, too, but Japan can hold its own."

"Oh, yeah. The Crab and the Monkey. I guess, now that you mention it. But Miyazaki and—why something from those parts?"

"Don't be asking me when you were attacked by a vampire in a backwater in Japan. It's not as if the location means anything, really. Given the right *situation*—it *arises there*, that's all."

Of course, geography and climate were important factors, Oshino supplemented.

"In this case, it doesn't even have to be a crab. Some say it's a rabbit or a beautiful woman—not to bring up little Shinobu."

"Huh, it's like the face of the Moon."

And hold on. He just called her "little Shinobu."

I felt a pang of sympathy for her, despite myself.

She was a legendary vampire, and yet…

How poignant.

"But since the young lady says she came across a crab, we must be dealing with a crab. That's standard, at the end of the day."

"What's that supposed to mean?" Senjogahara asked Oshino unshrinkingly. "What it's called is all the same to me, but—"

"I wouldn't say so. Names are important. As I just told Araragi, there aren't any crabs in the mountains of Kyushu. It might be different up north, but they'd be rare down south."

"You can probably find freshwater crabs, though," I noted.

"Maybe. But that's not the real issue here."

"Then what is?" demanded Senjogahara.

"It's that it may have originally been a god, not a crab. That *omoshi-kani* derives from *omoishi-gami*—but this is my personal theory. Most people think it's a crab first and the god bit is an afterthought. True, the straightforward view would be that they emerged simultaneously at the latest."

"'Most people'? 'Straightforward view'? I don't know of any such monster," Senjogahara objected.

"You wouldn't not know. After all," Oshino said, "*you've encountered it.*"

"……"

"And—*it's still right there.*"

"Are you saying *you—see something?*"

"*I don't. Not a thing,*" Oshino replied with an all too cheerful and lighthearted laugh that seemed, indeed, to bother Senjogahara.

As it did me.

Anyone would think he was mocking her.

"It's quite irresponsible of you to admit that you don't," Senjogahara said.

"Is that so? Spirits and such are basically invisible to the human eye. No one can see them or in any way touch them. That's the norm."

"That is—the norm."

"They say that ghosts don't have legs or that vampires don't show in mirrors, but that's not the point. Basically, *things* of their kind aren't identifiable in the first place. But I have a question for you, missy. Do *things* that no one can see or in any way touch really exist in this world?"

"You're asking me? You said yourself that it's right there."

"Why yes, I did. But isn't something that no one can see or in any way touch as good as nonexistent, scientifically speaking? Its being there and not being there are exactly the same."

That's what I mean, Oshino said.

Senjogahara hardly looked convinced.

It certainly wasn't a convincing line of reasoning.

Not from her standpoint.

"But, missy, consider yourself as being on the luckier side of misfortune. Araragi over there didn't just encounter something, he was attacked. By a vampire, at that. What a disgrace for a modern-day human being."

Get off my case, man.

As far off as you can.

"You're in fine shape compared to that, missy."

"And why is that?" Senjogahara asked.

"Because the gods are everywhere. They're everywhere, and they're nowhere. *It* was around you *before you became the way you are*—and we could just as well argue that *it* wasn't."

"That almost sounds like a Zen koan."

"It's Shinto. Maybe Shugendo," Oshino said. "You'd be wrong, missy, to think that you became *the way you are* because of *something* you did—it's just that your perspective shifted."

It was so from the beginning.

That—but that was barely any different from what the doctors who'd thrown in the towel maintained.

"My perspective? What are you trying to tell me?"

"I'm saying that I can't stand you playing the victim, missy," Oshino abruptly unleashed some harsh words.

Just like he'd done with me.

Or like he'd done with Hanekawa.

I was concerned about how Senjogahara would react—but she didn't reply.

It almost seemed like she was meekly accepting it.

"Huh." Oshino sounded impressed as he took in her state. "Not bad. I was sure you were some stuck-up princess."

"Why—did you think so?" Senjogahara asked.

"Because most people who encounter the Crab of Weight are *like that*. You don't come across it by choice, and it's normally not a harmful god. It's not like a vampire."

Not harmful?

It's not harmful—and doesn't attack?

"Nor does it actually possess people. It's there, that's all. Unless you, missy, have some wish, it doesn't manifest. Mind you, I'm not gonna dig that far into your circumstances. It's not as if I want to save you."

"……"

She was—going to get saved all on her own.

Oshino always said that.

"Stop me if you've heard this story, missy. It's a fairy tale from another country. There was once a youth. A virtuous lad. In town one day, he comes across a strange old woman, and she asks him to sell her his shadow."

"His shadow?"

"That's right. The very shadow that grows from your feet when you're in the sun. Sell it to me for ten pieces of gold, she said. The lad agreed without a moment's hesitation. For ten pieces of gold."

"…Then what happened?"

"What would you have done, missy?"

"Who knows—it's hard to say without being in that situation. I might sell it, and I might not. It would depend on the price, too."

"That's the right answer. People sometimes ask which is more valuable, your money or your life, but that's a flawed question. 'Money' could mean one yen, or it could mean a trillion, while on the other side, not all lives are equal across individuals. I utterly detest the vulgar dictum that all life is equal. But putting that aside—the lad couldn't imagine that his shadow was more valuable than ten pieces of gold. Why would he? In what way does not having a shadow inconvenience you? It wouldn't handicap you in any way."

Oshino continued, gesticulating. "But here's what happened as a result. The lad is persecuted by the townspeople and his own family. It creates discord with those around him who say—*it's creepy not to have a shadow*. Of course they would, because it really is. People talk about a creepy shadow, but not having any is much creepier. Something that ought to be there not being there—right? In other words, the lad sold what *ought to be* for ten pieces of gold."

"……"

"He searched for the old lady to get his shadow back but couldn't find her no matter how long or hard he tried—so tells the tale, flourish of music."

"And—" Senjogahara responded, her expression unchanged, "and what's your point?"

"Eh, there's no point. I just thought that, well, maybe it would strike a chord with you. The lad who sold his shadow and the lass deprived of her weight, you see?"

"It's not—as if I sold it."

"That's right. You didn't sell it. It was a barter. Losing your weight might be more inconvenient than losing your shadow, but in terms of not fitting in, it's the same. Still—is that all?"

"What do you mean?"

"Is that all, is what I mean." Oshino clapped his hands before his chest as if to say he was done with the topic. "Okay. Understood. You want to recover your weight, and I'll help. You obtained Araragi's introduction, after all."

"…You're going to—save me?"

"I'm not saving you. But I can help."

Let's see, Oshino said, checking the wristwatch on his left arm.

"The sun is still up, so go back home for now. Once you're there, cleanse your body with cold water and change into a clean set of clothes, okay? I'll make my own preparations in the meantime. Since you're classmates with Araragi, you must attend that buttoned-down school, but will you be able to leave home in the middle of the night?"

"I can do that much."

"Then can we say to meet here again at midnight?"

"Fine—but a clean set of clothes?"

"They don't have to be new, but your school uniform won't do. You wear it every day."

"…And your fee?"

"Huh?"

"Please don't play dumb. You're not saving me as an act of charity, are you?"

"Hm. Hrm." Oshino turned to look at me, appraisingly. "I guess I'll take one, missy, if that would make you feel better. All right, then, a hundred thousand yen."

"…A hundred thousand yen," Senjogahara parroted the sum. "A hundred thousand yen—huh."

"You can make that kind of money in a month or two working part-time at a fast food place. I think it's reasonable."

"…This is nothing like the treatment I got," I remarked.

"Was it not? I want to say that it was a hundred thousand yen for missy class president, too," Oshino countered.

"I'm saying that you charged me five million yen!"

"What do you expect? That was a vampire."

"Stop chalking everything up to vampirism! I hate when people rely on fads like that!"

Brushing away my complaints, Oshino asked Senjogahara, "Can you pay it?"

"Of course," she replied. "Of course, without fail."

And so—

And so now, two hours later, here we were.

At Senjogahara's home.

I took a look around—another one.

A hundred thousand yen isn't a small sum by normal standards, but her single-room abode made me think it was a particularly large one for Senjogahara.

There was nothing there other than the dresser, the low table, and a small bookshelf. Considering how voracious a reader she made herself out to be, her collection was meager, which meant she probably relied heavily on used bookstores and libraries.

Like the struggling student of yore.

Well, I guessed, that's actually what she was.

She said she was even on financial aid.

According to Oshino, Senjogahara got off easy compared to me—but I wasn't so sure.

Yes, being attacked by a vampire is no joke for the threat to your life and the trouble you end up causing. More than once I thought things would be easier if I were dead, and even now, after a single misstep, I find myself feeling that way.

So.

Maybe Senjogahara was on the luckier side of misfortune. But—given what Hanekawa had told me about Senjogahara the middle schooler, it felt wrong to box it up so tidily and see it that way.

The two weren't equal, to say the least.

Then a thought came to me.

Hanekawa—what about Hanekawa?

Tsubasa Hanekawa's case.

A woman whose first name meant "wing," and whose last name started with another character for the same, a pair of mismatched appendages.

Just as I was attacked by a demon and Senjogahara encountered a crab, Hanekawa was bewitched by a cat. That's what happened during Golden Week. It was so intense that it felt like the distant past as soon as it was over, but it had been just a few days.

Hanekawa, though, barely had any memories of Golden Week and seemed only to know that it was thanks to Oshino that she was fine, or maybe she knew nothing at all, but at any rate—I remembered everything.

It really was an awful case.

And that's coming from me, who had dealt with a demon at that point. I'd never imagined that a cat might be scarier than a demon.

So from the perspective of being life-threatening and all, you could simply say that Senjogahara's case was less dire than Hanekawa's—but considering what Senjogahara must have felt to get to where she was now...

Considering her current predicament.

If I did consider it.

What sort of life had gotten her to a place where generosity was deemed hostile behavior?

The lad who sold his shadow.

She who was deprived of her weight.

It was beyond me.

It wasn't for me to—understand.

"I'm done with my shower."

Senjogahara came out of the bathroom.

As naked as the day she was born.

"Gaaahhh!"

"Move out of the way. I can't get my clothes with you there." Coolly, annoyed with her wet hair, Senjogahara pointed to the drawer behind me.

"Clothes, put some clothes on!"

"That's what I'm trying to do."

"Why now?!"

"Are you saying I shouldn't?"

"I'm saying you should have already!"

"I forgot to bring them in with me."

"Then wear a towel or something!"

"No way, how classless," she pronounced with a serene expression.

It was clear as day that arguing with her would be futile, so I crawled out of the way of the dresser, toward the bookshelf, and focused my vision and my mind there as if to take inventory.

Urrgh.

I'd seen a fully nude woman for the first time…

B-But—something was wrong, it wasn't as I'd pictured it. While I don't think I harbored any illusions, what I'd wanted, what I'd dreamed of, wasn't this childlike streaking, this letting it all hang out…

"Clean clothes," she said. "Do you think white would be better?"

"Don't ask me…"

"I only own patterned underwear."

"Don't ask me!"

"I don't understand, why are you screaming like that when all I'm doing is asking you for advice? Are you going through menopause?"

The sound of a drawer being opened.

The rustling of clothes.

Ahh, too late.

The image was burned into my mind and wasn't going away.

"Araragi. Don't tell me you were sexually aroused at the sight of my nude body."

"Even if I was, it's not my fault!"

"Just try to lay a finger on me. I know that biting off your tongue will end the ordeal."

"Well, aren't you a chaste one!"

"I'm talking about your tongue, not mine."

"Okay, now you have me scared!"

I was starting to suspect that trying to understand this woman from my perspective was a fool's errand.

It's beyond humans to understand humans.

That should have been obvious.

"Okay. You can look now."

"Oh yeah? Sheesh…"

I turned away from the bookshelf and toward her.

She was still in her underwear.

She wasn't even wearing socks.

And she'd assumed a terribly provocative pose.

"What's your goal here?!" I yelled.

"Come on. This is my special thanks for helping me out today, so act at least a little happy."

"………"

It was her way of thanking me.

I didn't get it.

If anything, I wanted an apology more than any thanks.

"Act at least a little happy!"

"Now you're getting mad at me?!"

"It'd only be polite to provide some feedback."

"F-Feedback…!"

That would be polite?

What should I tell her?

Uhh…

"Like," I ventured, "Th-That's a nice body you've got there?"

"…I can't believe you," she spat with the kind of disgust reserved for piles of rotting garbage.

Actually, there was a bit of pity mixed in there, too.

"This is why you're a life-long virgin."

"Life-long?! Are you a time traveler or something?!"

"Could you please not spray your spittle? I might catch your virginity."

"Virginity is not something a woman can catch!"

Well, not that a man could, either.

"Hold on, we've been talking like it's a given that I'm a virgin!"

"Well, isn't it? No grade schooler would ever give you the time of day."

"I have two objections to that one! First, I'm not a pedophile, and second, some grade schooler somewhere would!"

"Why state the second point if the first is true?"

"……"

Why indeed.

"But you're right," she conceded. "I was jumping to conclusions."

"As long as you understand."

"Stop with the spittle. I might catch your except-for-pros virginity."

"In that case I admit that I'm a total cherry boy!"

Having cornered me into making a shameful confession, Senjogahara gave a satisfied nod. "You should've come out and said so from the start. This moment of happiness is easily worth half of your remaining lifespan, so just appreciate it."

"Are you the Grim Reaper or what…"

A deal to see a woman in the nude?

A new sort of evil eye.

"I wouldn't worry," Senjogahara assured as she took out and wore a white shirt over her aqua-blue bra. It seemed ridiculous to do another count of her books, so I just stared at her instead. "I wasn't going to tell

Hanekawa, you know?"

"Hanekawa?" I asked.

"Don't you have a crush on her?"

"Not true."

"Oh. I see you two talking all the time, so I was under that impression and thought I'd try a leading question."

"Keep leading questions out of everyday conversations."

"Shut up. Do you want to be disposed of?"

"Just what kind of authority are you purporting to be?"

Still, it seemed that Senjogahara was observing her classmates more than she let on. I'd wondered if she even knew that I was class vice president. No, actually, was this just another instance of her never knowing who might become her enemies one day?

"We talk all the time because she starts conversations with me," I explained.

"It sounds like you're forgetting your place. Are you trying to say that it's Hanekawa who has a crush on you?"

"Absolutely not," I said. "Hanekawa only does it because she's caring. Simply and overly caring. She has this funny, misguided notion that the worst loser in class is most in need of her sympathy. She thinks losers don't get enough of a break or something."

"You're right, how funny and misguided." Senjogahara nodded. "The worst loser is just the worst simpleton."

"…Hold on, I didn't go that far."

"It's written on your face."

"It isn't!"

"I knew you'd deny it, so I wrote that there a moment ago."

"You can't be that good at setting me up!"

In the first place—

Even without my clarifications, Senjogahara had to be familiar with Hanekawa's personality. When I spoke to Hanekawa after class, she sounded quite—concerned for Senjogahara.

Or maybe that was precisely the issue here.

"So—Mister Oshino helped Hanekawa out too?"

"Mm. I guess."

Senjogahara finished buttoning her shirt and was going for a white cardigan. She seemed to be figuring out the top half of her outfit before starting on the bottom. I see, I thought, so we all have our own way of dressing ourselves. Maybe my gaze didn't bother her one bit; she was facing toward me, if anything, as she continued to get dressed.

"Hmph," she said.

"So—I think it's all right to trust him. I know he doesn't act serious, and he's a happy-go-lucky, flippant, and frivolous guy, but one thing I can say about him is that he's good at what he does. You can relax. It's not just my testimonial, Hanekawa agrees, so there's no mistake."

"I see. But you know, Araragi, I'm sorry but I don't even half-trust Mister Oshino yet. I've been tricked far too many times to believe him just like that."

"……"

Five people—had tried similar lines on her.

All were frauds.

And—that probably wasn't the full extent of it.

"I visit the hospital out of habit, at this point. To be honest, I've all but resigned myself over the way my body is."

"Resigned…"

What did she resign herself—to?

What did she give up on?

"I can't expect to find any Van Helsings or Lord Darcys out there in our peculiar world."

I had no reply.

"Though you might find a useless, bumbling sidekick or two," she said in her most sarcastic tone. "Which is why, Araragi, I—couldn't possibly be so optimistic as to think that a classmate who *happened* to catch me when I *happened* to slip on the stairs *happened* to be attacked by a vampire over spring break, and that the man who *happened* to save you *happens* also to have been involved with the class president—and moreover *happens* to be willing to help me."

And then—

Senjogahara started taking off the cardigan.

"You finally put that thing on, so why are you taking it off now?"

"I forgot to dry my hair."

"Wait, could it be that you're just an idiot?"

"Please watch your mouth, Araragi? What if you hurt my feelings?"

Her hair dryer looked absurdly expensive.

It seemed she did pay a lot of attention to her getup.

Viewed from that angle, Senjogahara also seemed to be wearing fairly fashionable underwear, but that target of my adulation, so enchanting an overlord of the better part of my life until a day ago, somehow looked like no more than a scrap of cloth now. It felt as though a terrible trauma were being planted in me in the present participle tense.

"Optimistic, huh," I said.

"Don't you think?"

"Maybe. On the other hand, why not be optimistic?"

"……"

"It's not like you're doing anything wrong or cheating, so be unapologetic about it. Just like now."

"Like now?" Senjogahara looked puzzled. The lady didn't seem to realize how unflappable she was. "Hm—not doing anything wrong."

"Right?"

"I suppose."

Senjogahara wasn't done.

"But," she continued. "But—I might be cheating."

"Huh?"

"It's nothing."

She finished tending to her hair, put away her dryer, and turned to getting dressed again. She searched her drawer for new clothes, having placed on hangers the now-damp shirt and cardigan she'd worn with her hair still wet.

"If I'm reincarnated," Senjogahara said, "I'd like to be Sergeant Major Kululu."

"……"

Not only was this unprompted, but I felt her sadistic and self-centered behavior already put her halfway there…

"I know what you want to say," she accused. "Not only was that unprompted, but I could never in a million years?"

"Well, you got it half right."

"I knew it."

"…Couldn't you have at least said Lance Corporal Dororo?"

"For me, the words 'trauma switch' are too close for comfort."

"I see… But you know—"

"No ifs or bts."

"What the hell is a 'bts'?"

You couldn't even guess the word she'd maybe misspoken.

Naturally, I had no idea what she was trying to say, but even as I thought so, Senjogahara changed the subject.

"Hey, Araragi. Can I ask you something? Not that it really matters."

"Yeah."

"What did you mean by 'like the face of the Moon'?"

"Huh? What're you talking about?"

"You said it earlier, to Mister Oshino."

"Umm…"

Ah.

Right, I remembered.

"About the crab," I explained, "that guy Oshino said it can also be a rabbit or a beautiful woman. That's what I was talking about. People in Japan see rabbits in the moon, while in other countries they say it's a crab or a person's face."

Well, it's not that I see anything of the sort, but that's how the story goes.

"Got it." Senjogahara nodded along, perking up. "I'm surprised you know such a lame fact. You've managed to impress me for the first time ever."

She said lame.

She said the first time ever.

So I decided to double down.

"Well, I know a thing or two when it comes to astronomy and cosmology. I was really into it for a while."

"It's okay, you don't need to try to act smart with me. I already have you figured out. That's about the only thing you know, right?"

"You must think 'verbal abuse' is just a cute expression."

"Fine then, go ahead and call the verbal police."

"......"

I had a feeling that the real police wouldn't know what to do with her.

"Look," I insisted, "I'm not that clueless. Um, for example, in Japan it's a rabbit on the face of the Moon, but do you know why?"

"There aren't any rabbits on the Moon, Araragi. You're in high school and you still believe that?"

"Hypothetically speaking."

Wait. Hypothetically?

Did I mean figuratively?

This wasn't going so well…

"Once upon a time there was a god, or maybe it was the Buddha, but forget which, let's just say there was a god. For this god's sake, a rabbit chose to hop into a fire and to cook itself as a divine offering. Moved by its self-sacrifice, the god pinned its form up on the Moon in the sky so people would never forget the rabbit."

I was going off of some shaky knowledge salvaged from vague memories of a TV show I'd seen as a child, but I was sure those were the details.

"That was a cruel thing for the god to do," remarked Senjogahara. "It's like the rabbit got pilloried."

"No, it's not that kind of story."

"I don't know about that rabbit, either. Its transparent calculation that a display of self-sacrifice would win the god's recognition is almost grasping."

"It absolutely isn't that kind of story."

"In any case, it's not for the likes of me."

Having said this.

She started taking her top off again, her new one.

"…Are you just proud of your body and trying to show off or what?"

"I'm not so conceited as to be proud of my body. It was just inside out, and backwards, too."

"That's almost skilled."

"I will admit, wearing clothes isn't my forte."

"So you're like a kid."

"No, they're heavy."

"Ack."

That was thoughtless.

Right, if a bag felt heavy, clothes would too.

If everything had ten times the weight, your clothes were nothing to sneeze at.

I regretted it.

It was an insensitive—a careless thing to say.

"This," she said, "I might get tired of but never get used to—but you're actually quite erudite, Araragi. You've surprised me. There just might be some brain in that head of yours."

"Of course there is."

"Don't take things for granted… The cranium of an organism like you containing brain matter would be an event bordering on a miracle, all right?"

"Wow, that's a really mean thing to say."

"Don't let it bother you. I'm only stating facts here."

"I'd say someone in this room deserves to die…"

"What? Hoshina isn't here, though."

"Could you possibly have just claimed that a mentor to be respected, our homeroom teacher, deserves to die?!"

"Did the crab, too?"

"Huh?"

"Did it choose to hop into a fire, like the rabbit?"

"O-Oh… Well, I haven't come across anything about the crab. I wonder if there's a backstory. I never thought about it… Probably because the Moon has seas on it?"

"There aren't any seas on the Moon. How could you say that so smugly?"

"What? There aren't? Weren't there…"

"So much for your astronomy. They're not real seas, they're only called that."

"Oh…"

Hmmm.

I certainly couldn't hope to keep up with an actual smart person.

"Oh dear, Araragi, it seems you've shown your true colors. How rash of me to posit even for a moment that you possess any knowledge."

"You must think I'm really stupid."

"How did you figure that out?!"

"You look genuinely shocked!"

So she thought she was hiding it.

Really?

She lamented, "Because of me, Araragi, you've noticed how pitiful your mind is... I feel responsible."

"Hey, hold on, am I really that severely stupid?"

"Relax. Discriminating against people on account of their grades is something I'd never do."

"The way you phrased that is already setting off alarm bells!"

"Could you not spray your spittle? I might catch your truncated schooling."

"We go to the same high school!"

"Yes, but what about after that?"

"Urk..." She had me there.

"A graduate degree for me, while you're going to drop out of high school."

"I've made it to my senior year and I'm not quitting now!"

"Soon enough, you'll be crying and begging to be let off."

"A villain's line that I only ever hear in comics just rolls off your tongue?!"

"Let's compare test percentiles. Ninety-ninth for me."

"Guh..." She beat me to the punch. "Th-Thirty-fifth for me..."

"So zero, if you round."

"What?! Liar, a five gets... Wait, are you rounding by the tens?! How dare you do that to my percentile!"

She had more than sixty percentage points on me, she was beating a dead horse!

"I don't feel victorious until I'm up by a hundred points."

"You'd round yours by the tens, too..."

Merciless.

"So from now on, I don't want you coming within a 20,000-kilo-meter radius of me."

"Did you just order me off the face of the Earth?!"

"By the way, did the god do the rabbit the favor and actually feast on it?"

"Huh? Oh, you're back to that. Did he feast on it... If you pursued it that far, it would become a tale of the bizarre, okay?"

"It already is, pursued or not."

"Oh yeah? Why would I know, I'm stupid."

"Don't pout. You're gonna wreck my mood."

"Are you ever going to start feeling bad for me?"

"Pitying you alone won't rid the world of war."

"Don't be theorizing about the world when you can't even save a single human being! Start by helping the sad little life in front of you! I know you're up to it!"

"Hmph. All right, I've made up my mind," Senjogahara said, having dressed herself at last in a white tank top, a white jacket, and a white flared skirt. "If this all goes well, it's going to be crabs in Hokkaido."

"I'm pretty sure you can eat crabs without going all the way up to Hokkaido, and I don't think they're in season now, but sure, if that's what you want to do, be my guest."

"You're coming with me."

"Why?!"

"Oh, you didn't know?" Senjogahara smiled. "Crabs, Araragi, are delicious."

0 0 6

Our town in the provinces is also out in the country.

It gets incredibly dark at night. Pitch blackness. The contrast with daytime is such that the interior and exterior of an abandoned building becomes nearly indistinguishable.

For me, having lived here my entire life, that hardly feels off or strange, and really, that's how nature is supposed to work, but according to someone like Oshino, a drifter—the contrast tends to be entangled with the root of the *problem* more often than not.

It made the root easier to discern and comprehend—he told me that, too.

Either way.

It was now a little after midnight.

Senjogahara and I biked back to the cram school ruins. We used an actual cushion from Senjogahara's home for the rear seat.

I was mildly hungry, as I hadn't eaten anything.

When I parked my bike in the same spot I'd used in the evening and entered the grounds through the same hole in the fence, Oshino was there waiting for us at the entrance.

As if he'd been there for ages.

"Wha…" Senjogahara voiced surprise at his attire.

Oshino was wrapped in a white robe—a Shinto priest's. His scruffy hair was set neatly in place, and he at least looked tidier and was barely recognizable from the evening.

The robes make the man.

That he *somehow* looked the part was, actually, offensive.

"You were—a Shinto priest, Mister Oshino?" asked Senjogahara.

"What? Um, no?" he casually denied. "I'm no chief holy or ritualist. It's what I studied in school, but I never went to work for a shrine. I had too many objections."

"Objections…"

"Personal reasons. Maybe the truth is that it all started to seem silly to me. These clothes are just a way of dressing up for the occasion. I didn't have any other clean ones, that's all. We're going to meet a god, missy, so I have to look my best too. Didn't I tell you? Setting the mood. For Araragi, it was holding crosses, dangling garlic, and fighting with holy water. The situation is what matters. Don't worry, I might be lacking in manners, but I know what the deal is. I won't wave around a rod offhand or toss salt all over your head."

"O-Okay…"

Senjogahara seemed a bit daunted.

True, his outfit was striking, but coming from her, it seemed like a bit of an overreaction. It made me wonder.

"Yup, missy, you look clean and pure. Well done. Just to make sure, are you wearing any makeup?"

"No, I thought it would be better not to."

"I see. Well, for now, that was the right choice. And you, Araragi, you did take a shower?"

"Yeah, don't worry."

I hadn't had a choice since I was going to be present for this, and the little incident that ensued when Senjogahara tried to sneak a peek as I showered could stay a secret.

"Hmph. You, though, look your same old self."

"What's that got to do with anything?" I retorted.

I mean, even if I was going to be present, I was an outsider. Not having changed clothes too, unlike Senjogahara, of course I looked my same old self.

"Then let's get this over with. I've prepared a space on the third floor."

"A space?"

"Yep," Oshino said and disappeared into the darkness of the building. Despite his glaringly white robes, he was soon invisible. I took Senjogahara's hand just as I'd done in the evening and followed after him.

"You know, Oshino, you say 'over with' and are acting awfully laid back, but are you sure?"

"Sure? About what? I've summoned a boy and a girl of a tender age out here in the middle of the night. Any adult would want to finish up as quickly as possible."

"What I'm asking is if it'll be that easy to beat back this crab, or whatever it is."

"What a violent line of thought, Araragi. Something good happen to you?" Oshino shrugged without so much as turning around. "This time isn't like little Shinobu in your case or that lust-besotted cat in missy class president's. And don't forget, Araragi, I'm a pacifist. My basic policy is non-violent total obedience. You and missy class president were assaulted with malice and hostility. This crab is different."

"That's not true—" It'd done harm, in fact, so why not judge that it bore malice or hostility?

"Didn't I tell you? We're dealing with a god. It's just there and hasn't done anything. As a matter of course—it's just there. Araragi, once school is over for the day, you go home too, don't you? It's like that. Missy's been wavering all on her own."

It doesn't harm, it doesn't attack.

It doesn't possess.

"All on her own" sounded kind of mean, but Senjogahara said nothing. Did she simply have no thoughts pertaining to that, or was she, given what was to follow, trying not to react too much to his words?

"So Araragi," counseled Oshino, "whether it's beating back or up or down, lose those dangerous ideas. We're about to ask a god for a favor. Be humble."

"A favor, huh?"

"Right. A favor."

"And if we ask nicely, it's going to say here, and give it back?

Senjogahara's—weight. Her body weight."

"I won't say definitely, but probably. This isn't like spending New Year's Eve at a shrine. Well, they usually aren't so hard-headed as to turn down a sincere request. The gods are a fairly undiscerning bunch. Especially Japanese ones. Putting aside humans taken as a cluster, they couldn't care less about us on an individual basis. They really don't, okay? In fact, in face of a god, you, me, and missy over there are indistinguishable. Age, gender, weight, none of that matters, and all three of us are the same to them, humans."

We were—

Not just similar, but the same to them.

"Huh... So this is fundamentally different from a curse."

"Hey," Senjogahara said, her voice full of resolve, "is *that crab*—still near me?"

"It is. *It's there, and it's everywhere.* But if we *seek its advent here*— then certain steps will be necessary."

We arrived at the third floor.

We entered one of the classrooms.

A straw warding rope had been hung around the walls. The chairs and tables had been taken elsewhere, and an altar sat in front of the blackboard. Considering that the space was complete with stands filled with offerings, it couldn't have been slapped together after our earlier talk. Small lamps stood in each of the room's four corners and filled it with a dim light.

"Think of it as a spiritual field," Oshino explained. "The realm of divinity, as they say. It's nothing to get worked up about. You don't need to be so nervous, missy."

"I'm—not nervous."

"Is that so? Fantastic," Oshino said, proceeding into the classroom. "Could the two of you please lower your heads and cast down your eyes?"

"What?"

"We're already standing before a god."

Then—the three of us lined up in front of the altar.

These were nothing like the measures he took for me or Hanekawa

—speaking of nervous, I was the one feeling nervous. Such a stuffy mood—just this mood was making me feel funny.

My body shrank.

I couldn't help but be on guard.

I, myself, am one of those young, nonreligious kids nowadays who can't distinguish between Shintoism and Buddhism. And yet my heart was home to some instinct or other that reacted to this very situation.

Situation.

Space.

"Hey—Oshino."

"What is it, Araragi?"

"I was just thinking, if this is about the situation and space, should I even be here? However you think of it, I'm an intruder."

"You aren't exactly intruding. Everything should be fine, but you never know, stuff happens. Stuff can always happen. And if it does, Araragi, you're going to act as a wall for missy."

"I am?"

"What else is that immortal body of yours good for?"

"……"

Well, that certainly was a cool line, but I was pretty sure it wasn't to act as a wall for Senjogahara.

To begin with, I wasn't immortal anymore.

"Araragi," Senjogahara pleaded without missing a beat, "promise you'll protect me."

"Why a princess character all of a sudden?!"

"What's the big issue? You must be planning to off your worthless self as soon as tomorrow anyway."

"Out of character in nothing flat!"

Moreover, words that were hardly whispered behind your back in your lifetime had been spoken straight to my face like normal. Being on the receiving end of her acid tongue made me wonder if I needed to give serious thought to the evils I'd wrought in a past life.

"Of course, I'm not asking you to do this for free," she said.

"You gonna gimme something?" I asked.

"How shallow of you to seek a material reward. It wouldn't be a stretch to say that your entire humanity is summarized by that sad little response."

"……Then whacha gonna do for me?"

"Hmm… You're scum who tried to equip the slave outfit to Nera in *Dragon Quest V*, but I'm going to halt my plans to spread the word."

"I've never even heard of anyone doing that!"

Plus, spreading the word was her premise.

What a horrible woman.

"It should have been obvious that you can't equip it to her… That's just so harebrained, or should I say 'dogbrained'?"

"Hold on a second! You're looking triumphant like that was a witty insult, but have I once been compared to a dog in any way?!"

"Right," Senjogahara snickered. "How unfair of me. To dogs."

"………rk!!"

Weaving in, at that moment, an old standby that would otherwise sound hackneyed… This woman had complete mastery over all things insulting.

"Fine, then, forget it," she said. "A coward like you can run home with your tail between your legs and play lonely games with a taser like you do every night."

"What sort of perverted play is that?!"

Or rather, stop spreading one insidious rumor after another about me.

"When you're on my level, Araragi, it's easy to see through a flimsy little thing like you. I know all of your dorkest secrets."

"How did you manage to misspeak and come up with an even worse insult?! What the hell are you the beloved of?!"

She was unfathomable in that respect.

She must have meant to say "darkest."

"Anyway, Oshino," I reprised. "Why ask me? Won't that vam—Shinobu do? Like that time with Hanekawa."

He simply replied, "It's past her bedtime."

"………"

A vampire sleeping at night?

It really was poignant.

Oshino took a vessel of sake from the offerings and handed it to Senjogahara.

"Hm? What now?" she asked, confused.

"Drinking alcohol can bring you closer to the gods—apparently. Go ahead, in the way of loosening up."

"...I'm a minor."

"You don't have to go so far as to get drunk. Just a teeny sip."

"......"

After a moment of hesitation, Senjogahara did gulp down a mouthful as he watched. She handed back the vessel to Oshino, who returned it to its original location.

"Okay. Let's calm down," Oshino said, still facing forward—his back to Senjogahara. "We'll start by calming down. The situation is what matters. As long as we create a space, manners don't—it's all up to your frame of mind in the end, missy."

"My frame of mind..."

"Relax. Start by letting your guard down. This place is yours. It's natural for you to be here. Keeping your head lowered and closing your eyes—let's count. One, two, three..."

Really—

There was no need for me to, but I found myself following along, closing my eyes and counting. As I did, it came to me.

Setting the mood.

In that sense, not just Oshino's attire, but the straw warding rope, the altar, and even the trip home to bathe were all requirements for setting the mood—or, to take it further, setting up Senjogahara's mental condition.

It was close to suggestion.

Hypnotic suggestion.

Begin by wiping away her self-consciousness, get her to lower her guard, bring about a relationship of trust with him—although he was going about it in a completely different way, it had been no less necessary for me and Hanekawa. They say believe and you shall be saved, and getting Senjogahara to *accept*, in a nutshell—was crucial.

Senjogahara had said it herself.

She didn't even half-trust Oshino yet.

But—

That wouldn't cut it.

That wouldn't be enough.

Because—a relationship of trust was required.

Oshino couldn't save Senjogahara, she was getting saved on her own—that was the true meaning of his words.

I slowly opened my eyes.

I looked around.

Lamps.

The lamp flames in the corners—wavered.

A wind blew in from the windows.

Shaky flames—that could be snuffed out at any moment.

Yet their light was certain.

"Do you feel calm?"

"—Yes."

"All right—then let's answer some questions. You've decided to answer my questions. Missy, what's your name?"

"Hitagi Senjogahara."

"What school do you go to?"

"Naoetsu Private High School."

"What's your birthday?"

"July seventh."

A Q&A whose meaning wasn't clear, that in fact seemed totally meaningless, unfolded.

Flatly.

At a steady pace.

Oshino still had his back to Senjogahara.

She, too, hid her face, her eyes closed.

Her head lowered, downcast.

It felt quiet enough for breaths and heartbeats to make themselves heard.

"Who's your favorite author?"

"Kyusaku Yumeno."

"How about an embarrassing story from when you were a kid?"

"I don't want to tell."

"What kind of classical music do you like?"

"I'm not very well-versed in music."

"How did you feel when you graduated elementary school?"

"Only that I would be attending middle school next. Because I was just going from one public school to another."

"What was the boy who was your first love like?"

"I don't want to tell."

"In your life so far," Oshino said in the same steady tone, "what experience hurt the most?"

"………"

Here—Senjogahara drew a blank.

Not even an "I don't want to tell"—but silence.

I realized then that Oshino had imbued just this question with meaning.

"What's the matter? The most hurtful experience in your life. I'm asking you about your memories."

"…M."

The mood—wasn't one where she could remain silent.

She couldn't refuse with an "I don't want to tell."

That—was the situation.

The space that had been formed.

According to plan—things moved forward.

"My mother—"

"Your mother…"

"Falling for a bad religion."

She'd fallen for some sketchy new religion.

Senjogahara had told me.

That her mother gave them everything they owned and even took on debt, until their family fell apart. That even after the divorce, her father still worked around the clock to pay off the loans.

Was that—the experience that hurt her the most?

More than—being deprived of her weight?

Of course it was.

How could it not hurt worse.

But—that…

That…

"*That's all?*" Oshino asked.

"…What do you mean?"

"If that's all, it's no big deal. Freedom of faith is recognized by the laws of Japan. No, freedom of faith is recognized as an authentic human right. What your mother reveres or prays to is merely an issue of methodology."

"………"

"*So—that's not all,*" Oshino asserted forcefully. "Try and tell. What happened?"

"Like I said—m-my mother—because of me she fell for such a religion—she got duped—"

"Your mother was duped by a cult—*then what.*"

Then what.

Senjogahara bit down hard on her lower lip.

"A-An executive member of the religious group came to our house with my mother."

"An executive member. This person came, and then?"

"H-He said it would be purifying."

"Purifying? It'd be purifying? He said it'd be purifying—and then?"

"He said it was a ritual—he *took—me* and," Senjogahara said, pain mixing into her voice, "a-assaulted me."

"Assault—in the sense of getting violent? Or—in a sexual sense?"

"In the sexual—sense. Yes, that man—" Senjogahara continued as if she were enduring a variety of things, "*tried to rape me.*"

"…I see."

Oshino nodded—quietly.

Senjogahara's—

Fixation on chastity that took an unnatural form, her—

Cautiousness.

The highly defensive mentality and acutely aggressive mindset.

It felt like they made sense now.

So did her excessive reaction to Oshino's ritual garb.

For a non-pro like Senjogahara, the fact was that Shintoism, too, was a *religion*.

"That—hypocritical lecher—"

"That's the Buddhist perspective. A religion can even endorse killing one of your own. It won't do to generalize. But you said *tried to rape*—so it ended at an attempt?"

"I hit him with my cleats which were nearby."

"…That was brave."

"He bled from his forehead—and was writhing on the floor."

"And that saved you?"

"It saved me."

"Good for you."

"*But—my mother didn't try to save me.*"

Even though she was there the entire time, watching—Senjogahara said flatly.

Flatly she continued with her answer.

"In fact—she scolded me."

"That's—all?"

"No—because I injured that leader, my mother—"

"Your mother was *penalized*?" Oshino finished Senjogahara's line for her.

The consequences of such a scene didn't take an Oshino to predict—but this seemed to have an effect on her.

"Yes," she affirmed—solemnly.

"Naturally—since her daughter injured one of the leaders."

"Yes. And so—everything we had. The house, the land—even going into debt—my family broke. Completely broke—it completely broke, and yet, it continues to fall apart. It continues to, sir."

"How is your mother doing now?"

"I don't know."

"There's no way that you don't."

"She's probably—still practicing her faith."

"Still."

"Not having learned a thing—unashamed."

"Does that hurt, too?"

"It does—hurt."

"Why does it hurt? She has nothing to do with you anymore."

"Sometimes I wonder. What if, at the time, I—*hadn't resisted*, then at least—it might not have gotten to this."

It might not have broken.

It might not have broken.

"You think so?" asked Oshino.

"I do—think so."

"You really think so."

"...I do."

"Then *that*, missy—is *your thought and burden*," Oshino said. "*No matter how weighty*, it's what you need to shoulder. *Leaving it to someone else*—isn't the way to go."

"Leaving it to someone else—isn't—"

"Don't avert your eyes—*open them and take a look.*"

Then—

Oshino opened his eyes.

Senjogahara also opened her eyes—gently.

The lamps in the corners.

Their light wavered.

The shadows, too.

All three of our shadows also—wavered.

They swayed back and forth.

Back—and forth.

"Ah. Ahhhhh!"

Senjogahara—yelled.

She was still managing to keep her head lowered—but her expression was filled to overflowing with shock. Her body was trembling, and began to gush sweat.

She was losing it.

Her—Senjogahara.

"Do you—see something?" questioned Oshino.

"I-I do. It's like that time—like that time, a huge crab, a crab—I see it."

"Do you, now. Well, I don't see a thing."

It was then that Oshino turned for the first time, toward me.

"Do you see anything, Araragi?"

"I—don't."

There was nothing to see.

Only the wavering light.

And wavering shadow.

That was—the same as not seeing.

I couldn't identify it.

"I don't see—a thing."

"You heard him." Oshino turned toward Senjogahara. "I bet you don't see any crab, actually?"

"N-No—it's visible. Clearly. *To me.*"

"It's not an illusion?"

"It isn't an illusion—I mean it."

"I see. Then—"

Oshino traced Senjogahara's line of sight.

As if something—were there.

As if some thing—were there.

"Then, what do you need to say to it?"

"Need to—say."

That's when it happened.

I doubt she had any reason at all, but.

She couldn't have meant anything by it, but.

Senjogahara—raised her head.

It was probably the situation.

The space had become too much for her.

That must have been all.

But circumstances didn't matter.

Paltry, human circumstance didn't matter.

The very same moment—Senjogahara leapt backward.

She flew.

Like she had no weight to speak of, her feet not once touching or dragging across the floor, she sped to the very back of the classroom, opposite from the altar, and *was slammed* into the bulletin board.

Slammed into it—

She stayed there and didn't drop.

She didn't drop.

As if she'd been pinned up, she stayed there.

As if it were a crucifixion.

"S-Senjogahara!"

"Oh boy," Oshino said, dismayed. "I thought I told you to act as her wall, Araragi. Once again, you're useless when it counts the most. Spacing out like a literal wall can't be all you're good for."

Dismaying or not, I couldn't help it because her velocity had outpaced my eyes.

As if gravity were functioning in that vector, Senjogahara seemed to be pressed, shoved against the bulletin board.

Her body—began to burrow into the wall.

It looked ready to crack and fall apart.

Or Senjogahara was about to be crushed.

"Uh... U-Ugh..."

It wasn't a scream—but a groan.

She was in pain.

Yet—I still didn't see a thing.

All I saw was Senjogahara pinning herself, seemingly, to the wall. However. However, though—she must have been seeing it.

A crab.

A large—crab.

The Crab of Weight.

"So much for that. Sheesh, what an impatient god, couldn't even wait for us to start praying. How so game of it. Wonder if something good happened to it."

"H-Hey, Oshino—"

"Yeah, I know. Change of plans. Too bad, but this is quite standard. Either way was fine for me from the beginning."

Saying so with a sigh, but with a sure gait, Oshino approached Senjogahara's crucified body.

Approached her without ado.

Then, his hand reached out casually.

It *took hold slightly in front of* Senjogahara's face.

Easily—peeled away.

"Hup."

In one motion, as if he were performing a judo throw—Oshino took *the thing* he had in his hand and forcefully, with all his might—slammed it against the floor. There was no sound, no swirl of dust. But he slammed it *just as Senjogahara had been, only stronger.* Then swiftly, in the very same breath, he stepped on this slammed *it*.

He was stepping on a god.

In a consummately violent manner.

Irreverently, without an ounce of deference or piety.

The pacifist made light of a god.

"......gk."

To me, it only looked as if Oshino had mimed everything—performed an incredibly expert pantomime, as he still was now, seemingly balancing himself on one leg with aplomb. Meanwhile, for Senjogahara, who could see *it* very well—

It was apparently the sort of sight that made her eyes grow wide.

It's apparently that sort of sight.

But a second later, no doubt having lost her support, she went from being pinned to the wall to splatting onto the floor. Since she wasn't too high up and had no weight, the impact of the fall couldn't have been too severe, but she couldn't brace for it, having dropped completely by surprise. It looked like she'd hit her leg hard.

"You okay?" Oshino called to check up on Senjogahara before looking down at his own feet. Indeed—purely appraisingly.

Evaluating, with narrowed eyes.

"No matter how big a crab gets, in fact the bigger it is, turn it upside down, and there you go. Whatever the creature, if it has a flat body, I can't help but think that it exists to be stepped on, looking at it sideways or any other way—that said, Araragi, what do you think?" Oshino abruptly addressed me. "We certainly could redo this from the beginning, but it'd be such a hassle. Personally, it'd be neatest for me to go on and squish and squash it."

"Neatest? A-And 'squish and squash' is awfully vivid... She only raised her head for a moment. Just that—"

"I wouldn't call it just that. Or rather, just that is enough. In the end, this stuff is about your frame of mind—if we can't be nice and ask a favor, then we have to resort to dangerous ideas. Like when we dealt with the demon or the cat. *If we can't talk, then there's only war*—okay? In a sense it's just like politics. Well, simply crushing it would solve missy's problems on a surface level. It'd be only on the surface, a palliative treatment that doesn't touch the root, just mowing the weeds, so to speak, a method I'm not eager to take, but maybe on this occasion I should just go for it."

"G-Go for it?"

"You see, Araragi," Oshino said with a disquieting grin, "I absolutely despise crabs."

They're hard to eat, he explained.

And with those words—

With those words, his leg—flexed.

"Wait."

The voice came from behind Oshino.

Needless to say, it was Senjogahara.

Rubbing her skinned knee, she sat up.

"Wait—please. Mister Oshino."

"Wait for—" Oshino shifted his gaze from me to Senjogahara, the malicious smile still on his face. "Wait for what, missy?"

"I was just—surprised earlier," Senjogahara said. "I can do this. On my own."

"…Hunh."

Oshino wasn't pulling back his leg.

He kept stepping on it.

But not squashing it either, he told Senjogahara, "Fine, give it a try."

Told this—

Utterly unbelievably, from my point of view, Senjogahara knelt, righted her posture, placed her hands on the floor—towards *it* at Oshino's feet, and slowly—properly bowed her head.

She was—prostrating herself.

Hitagi Senjogahara—was performing a *dogeza* of her own will.

Assuming the pose freely, unbidden.

"—I'm sorry."

She began with words of apology.

"And—thank you very much."

She followed up with words of gratitude.

"But—it's all right now. They're—my feelings, my thoughts—and my memories, so I will shoulder them. It wasn't right of me to lose them."

And then, finally—

"Please. I beg of you to grant me this favor. Please, give me back my weight."

Finally, words of supplication, as if she were praying.

"Please give me back—my mother."

Wham.

It was the sound of Oshino's foot—hitting the floor.

Not from squashing the thing, I presumed.

No, it had vanished.

Just as it simply was—it must have returned from being there as a matter of course back to not being there as a matter of course.

Sent back.

"Ah—"

At Mèmè Oshino, who stood unspeaking, unmoving.

At Hitagi Senjogahara, who maintained her posture despite knowing it was over and who began sobbing, wailing out loud.

Standing apart and gazing at them, Koyomi Araragi vacantly, vacuously wondered: Ah, maybe Senjogahara is a *tsundere* through and through and through.

0 0 7

The timeline.

I had misconstrued the timeline.

I was sure that Senjogahara encountering the crab and losing her weight had eaten away at her mother, who then fell for the money-grubbing sect—but I was told that in reality, her mother had fallen for it long before Senjogahara ever encountered the crab and lost her weight.

I should've been able to figure that out with some thought.

Unlike stationery tools like box cutters and staplers, cleats aren't something you just happen to reach out and find nearby. That word coming up should have tipped me off then and there that Senjogahara had been on the track team at the time—that she'd been in middle school. There was no way she could have been in high school when even gym classes were off limits and she belonged to the no-extracurriculars club.

Apparently, the exact point at which her mother fell for the religion—started to believe in it—was when Senjogahara was in fifth grade. Back in elementary school, before even Hanekawa knew her.

And according to Senjogahara.

In those days—she was a girl who was always ill.

Not as her positioning, but as a matter of fact.

Then, at a certain point, she was stricken with a terrible sickness that everyone has heard of. Her condition was such that she had only one chance out of ten of surviving and doctors indeed wanted to throw in the towel.

That's when—

Senjogahara's mother began looking for solace.

Or should we say, was taken advantage of.

Probably totally unrelated to that—though "No one can know for sure whether or not it was unrelated," Oshino opined—Senjogahara underwent major surgery and managed to be that one out of ten. The faint surgery scar that supposedly remained on her back was another thing I might have noticed, had I observed her nude body in detail at her home, but demanding that of me would border on cruel.

I do admit that accusing her of just trying to show off her body when she started dressing herself from the top down, facing me head-on, was indeed cruel.

Some feedback at least, she'd said.

In any case, thanks to Senjogahara's recovery, her mother—only became more absorbed with the religion's teachings.

Because of her piety—her daughter had been saved.

She'd fallen for a classic trap.

It's what you might call a symptomatic case.

Still, the household itself—somehow persisted. I have no way of knowing what kind of creed of what group this was, but not bleeding its believers dry—had to be their basic policy at least. Senjogahara's father's ample income and their family starting out affluent certainly helped—but as the years went on, her mother's piety, her absorption, only worsened in degree.

The household was merely persisting.

Senjogahara's relationship with her mother began to sour.

It was one thing up through the time she graduated from elementary school—but after she began middle school, they barely spoke. Looking back, with that in mind, at what I learned from Hanekawa about Senjogahara's middle-school persona is to understand just how warped it was.

Really, it was like—an attempt at vindication.

Superhuman.

In middle school, Senjogahara was almost superhuman.

And—maybe it was to assure her mother: I can do this, we don't need any religion.

As much as their relationship had soured.

She probably never was an active girl, at heart.

If she was always ill in grade school, then even more so.

She must have been forcing it.

But it was, more likely than not, counterproductive.

A vicious circle.

The better she did, and the more exemplary she became—the more her mother must have thanked the religion's teachings.

The counterproductive, vicious circle wound on—

Her third year of middle school.

It happened when graduation was around the corner.

Originally having joined for her daughter's sake, somewhere along the way Senjogahara's mother's logic got flipped around to the point that she was offering her daughter to one of the cult's executive members. No, maybe that, too, was for her daughter's sake—the thought is too much to bear.

Senjogahara resisted.

With her cleats she wounded the leader badly enough that he bled from his forehead.

As a result—

Their family fell apart.

It was in ruins.

Robbed wholesale.

Losing everything they owned, their home, their land—and even taking on debt.

They were all but literally bled dry.

Although the divorce was only finalized last year according to Senjogahara, and it must have been as a high school student that she started to live in the Tamikura Apartments, it was already all over when she was in middle school.

All over.

That's why.

That's why Senjogahara—during that halfway period between being a middle schooler and a high schooler—came across it.

A crab.

"You see, Araragi. The *omoshi-kani* is an *omoishi-gami*," Oshino said. "Do you understand? *Omoishi* as in 'thinking upon,' and *omoi* and *shigami* as in 'thoughts' and 'clinging'—it has to do with inextricable bonds, *shigarami*. Doesn't interpreting it that way explain why being deprived of weight also deprives people of their presences? People sealing away a memory when they've gone through too much is common fare in dramas and movies. If you want an analogy, that would be it. It's a god that carries people's thoughts in our place."

In other words, when she met the crab…

Senjogahara—cut off her mother.

She had offered Senjogahara to the leader like some sacrifice and not even tried to save her daughter, causing their family to fall apart, except maybe that wouldn't have happened if the daughter hadn't resisted at the time—Senjogahara had tormented herself. Then she quit.

She stopped thinking about it.

She rid herself of that weight.

Freely, on her own.

She had—cheated.

She had sought—solace.

"It's a barter. A trade, equivalent exchange. Crabs are clad in armor and look durable, don't they? That's probably the idea here. Put a shell around your exterior. Preserve what's dear, enveloping it with an exoskeleton. All the while bubbling foam that vanishes right away. I won't have them."

He wasn't kidding about not fancying crab.

Although he seemed flippant, Oshino was actually—kind of gauche.

"The character for 'crab' is made up of the ones for 'solving' and 'insect,' isn't it? It's a critter that breaks things down. Organisms that crisscross edges of water tend to fall under that rubric. What's more, those guys are—equipped with scissors, two pairs at that."

As a result.

Senjogahara was deprived of her weight—losing it, losing her thoughts, she was liberated from her suffering. Free of torment—she was able to give it all up.

And when she did?

She said things got—much easier.

That was her honest feeling.

In and of itself, being deprived of her weight wasn't a big deal for Senjogahara. Yet—even so, like the lad who sold his shadow for ten pieces of gold, there wasn't a day that it, *things being easier*, didn't gnaw at her.

But not because of any discord with others.

Not because of any inconvenience in going about her life.

Not because she can't make any friends.

Not because she lost everything.

Simply because—she lost her thoughts, her burden.

The five frauds.

None of them seems to have anything to do with her mother's religion—but even as Senjogahara only half-trusts the bunch, Oshino included, she lends them close to half of her trust—and you can say, that, there, is her expression of regret. Not to mention visiting the hospital out of sheer habit—

There's nothing to it.

I got it all wrong, from the very start to the very end.

All this time after being deprived of her weight, Senjogahara—

Hasn't resigned herself.

Hasn't given up on anything.

"It's not necessarily bad, you know," Oshino argued. "Confronting a painful experience isn't a must. It's not like you're great just 'cause you do. If you don't feel like it, it's totally fine to run away. Even if it's ditching your daughter or taking refuge in religion, that's your own choice. Especially in this case, getting back your thought and burden at this late stage won't do a thing, right? Missy, who stopped feeling tormented, will torment herself again, but that won't bring back her mother or restore her wrecked family."

Won't do a thing.

Oshino seemed to intend that as neither ridicule nor sarcasm.

"The *omoshi-kani* robs you of your weight, your thinking, your presence. But it's not like our little vampire Shinobu or that lust-besotted cat. Missy *hoped for it*, so it in fact *dispensed*. A barter—the god was always there. Missy actually hadn't lost a thing. In spite of that…"

In spite of that.

Regardless of that.

Because of that.

Hitagi Senjogahara—wanted it returned.

She wanted it returned.

Her thinking of her mother, after the fact.

The memory and the torment.

I don't know what that means, and I doubt I ever will, and just as Oshino pointed out, it's neither here nor there and won't bring her mother or her family back, and it will only steep Senjogahara in tormented thoughts, but—

It's not like anything is going to change, but.

"It's not like nothing is going to change," Senjogahara said at the end.

To me, her eyes red and swollen from crying.

"And this definitely wasn't pointless. Because I've made a very dear friend, at least."

"Who would that be?"

"I'm talking about you."

I'd reflexively played dumb, but Senjogahara's response was neither bashful nor roundabout, but forward—and proud.

"Thank you, Araragi. I'm very grateful for what you've done. I apologize for everything until now. I hope you don't find this brazen of me, but I'd be very happy if we could continue to be friends."

How careless of me—

This surprise attack by Senjogahara seeped deep into my heart, deep.

Our promise to go eat crabs, though?

It's going to have to wait until winter.

008

The epilogue, or maybe, the punch line of this story.

The next day, when I was roused from bed as usual by my little sisters Karen and Tsukihi, my body felt horribly sluggish. It was an ordeal just forcing myself to sit up, then stand. My joints ached heavily like when you have a high fever. Since there hadn't been any tussle or brawl unlike my time or Hanekawa's, it couldn't be muscle pain, but at any rate, every step hurt. Walking down the stairs, too, I was afraid I might tumble down them if I didn't pay attention. My mind was clear, and it wasn't flu season, either, so what was going on?

I thought for a bit before an improbable thought crossed my mind.

I made a detour to the bathroom on my way to the kitchen.

In it is a scale.

I got on.

I weigh fifty-five kilograms, by the way.

The scale read a hundred.

"…Hey, hey."

So it's true.

The gods surely are an undiscerning bunch.

CHAPTER TWO
MAYOI SNAIL

001

I encountered Mayoi Hachikuji on May fourteenth, a Sunday. This day was Mother's Day across Japan. Whether you love your mother or not, whether you get along with your mother or not, the day is Mother's Day for every Japanese person alike. I want to say that Mother's Day originated in America. In that sense, it may be best to consider it a kind of event, like Japan does Christmas, Halloween, Valentine's Day, and the like. But in any case, of all three hundred and sixty-five days of the year, this day, May fourteenth, was the one where more carnations were sold than any other, and when coupons promising the delivery of back rubs, chores, and so on were trading hands in homes across the country. Well, I don't really know if those kinds of customs are still being observed, but I am sure that May fourteenth was indeed Mother's Day this year.

And it was on that day.

That day, at nine in the morning.

I was sitting on a bench in an unfamiliar park. I was staring up into the sky like an idiot at an idiotically blue sky, nothing to do as I sat on a bench in an unfamiliar park. I was more than unfamiliar with it, I'd never even heard of it. But it was a park.

Namishiro Park, a sign at its entrance stated.

Well, maybe it did. The way it's written I barely have any idea how it's supposed to be read, whether those characters say "Namishiro Park," "Rohaku Park," or something else entirely different. Maybe there's some reason behind its name, but of course I don't know it. It's not as if that's any kind of issue, of course. Not knowing the park's name doesn't affect me at all. I didn't go to the park with any sort of firm goal in mind, but was riding my mountain bike in whatever direction my feelings and legs took me until I found myself arriving at the park. That's all, and nothing more.

I didn't go to visit the park, I arrived there.

Though of course, the difference was meaningless to anyone other than myself.

I'd put my bike in the parking area near the entrance.

There were two objects in the lot that had been so abandoned and so exposed to the elements that you couldn't tell whether they were supposed to be bicycles or clumps of rust, and then there was my mountain bike. Other than that, it was completely empty. It was one of those moments when I really felt the futility of riding around the asphalt streets on a mountain bike, but it was also a futility I felt at all times, whether I was doing something like that or not.

It was a fairly big park.

While I say that, it might have only felt that way because of how few objects there were to play with inside. It only looked wide open. Swings on one edge of the park, and a tiny little sandbox, but that was it. No seesaw, no jungle gym, not even a slide. Perhaps parks should have inspired in my high-school-senior self a greater sense of nostalgia, but I can't deny I was feeling quite the opposite of that.

Or maybe that's how things were. This was what you got when you gave thought to how dangerous playground structures were and how to keep children safe, and it came to look this way after all the old playthings had been removed. My opinion of the place wouldn't have changed even if that were the case, and I'd personally think the swings were the most dangerous of all, but putting that aside, part of me keenly felt what a miracle it was that I was still of sound body.

I'd done a lot of reckless things as a child, after all.

It wasn't nostalgia I felt as I thought these things.

Then again.

You could say that my body was no longer of sound health as of about a month and a half before May fourteenth—but I guess whatever wounded sentiment lay in my heart had yet to fully process the fact. Honestly, it wasn't the kind of thing you could sort out in a couple of months. An entire lifetime might not be enough.

But, I thought.

Even without the missing play structures, the park was such a lonely place. I mean, I was completely alone there. Even though it was a Sunday, that greatest of days. The lack of things to play on meant the place felt larger, so grab a ball and a bat and play some baseball, I thought. Or maybe, I wondered, elementary schoolers these days no longer defaulted to baseball, then soccer, when they wanted to go have fun. They probably played video games all day at home—or they were busy going to cram school? Either that, or all the kids in the area were faithful little sons and daughters who spent the entire day celebrating Mother's Day.

But even then, being all alone in a park on Sunday almost made it feel like I was the only person left on Earth—well, that would be an exaggeration, but it did feel that the park belonged to me. Like I never had to go home again. Because it was all me, I was all alone...or not? There was one other person after all. I wasn't all alone. A large open space separated my bench from someone at a metal sign at the edge of the park—a lone grade schooler who was looking at a residential map of the area. The child's back was facing me, so I had no idea what he or she was like, but the large backpack the kid carried was notable. My heart warmed for a moment like I'd found a new buddy, but the grade schooler spent a while looking at the map, then ran off, as if remembering something. And then I was alone.

By myself. Again.

I thought.

—You know, Koyomi.

That's when I randomly thought—of my little sister's words to me.

The casual words she tossed at my back as I left home on my mountain bike.

—You know, Koyomi, that's why—

Ah.

Dammit, I thought, as I switched from my earlier position of staring at the sky to gazing straight at the ground, head in my hands.

I felt a wave of depression rolling over me.

I'd been quite calm as I looked up into the sky, but now, of all times, I found myself hating how petty I was. I suppose the feeling was what you'd call self-loathing—while I was not normally the type to be bothered by that sort of thing, in fact, it was rare I had any thoughts at all I'd describe as bothering me, I would on rare occasions, on event days like this one, the fourteenth of May, fall into such a state. Special circumstances, unique setups. I was horribly susceptible to them. They made me lose my composure. They made me restless.

Oh, there's nothing better than a weekday.

Can't it be tomorrow already?

And it was in this odd state—that my episode involving a snail began. Or if you look at it the other way around, the episode probably wouldn't have so much as started if I hadn't been in such a state.

0 0 2

"My goodness, look at what we have here. I thought someone had dumped a dead dog on a park bench, but it was just you, Araragi."

I raised my head, as I thought I heard a greeting so novel it may have been used for the first time in human history, and saw my classmate Hitagi Senjogahara standing there.

This goes without saying, but she was not in her school uniform, as it was Sunday. I began wondering how I should reply to suddenly being called a dead dog, but her standing there in casual clothes, wearing her straight hair up in a ponytail instead of down as she does in school, was such a fresh sight that I couldn't stop myself from swallowing the words that had made it all the way up to my throat.

Wow...

It's not as if she was showing off that much skin, but her outfit seemed to draw attention to her chest in an inexplicable way—not to mention the culottes she wore, which would have been unthinkably short were it part of her school uniform. It wasn't even a proper skirt, but her black stockings only made her legs that much more seductive.

"What's the matter? It's a greeting, that's all. A joke. I wish you wouldn't look like such a wet blanket, Araragi. Are you sure you have anything resembling a sense of humor?"

"Ah, n-no, it's..."

"Or can it be that your innocent little heart is smelted by my charming appearance, and that you're experiencing a moment of bliss?"

"………"

She was so spot-on, or at least close enough to being right that I couldn't come up with a good retort despite her odd word choice.

"Isn't that such a wonderful word, 'smelt'? They say it has the same roots as the word 'melt,' but it's so much more intense. I mean, you can melt just about anything, but smelting places itself a notch above, and people have high hopes for it as an emotive next-gen term. 'That maid smelted my heart!' or 'I smelt for cat ears!' and that sort of thing."

"…I was surprised by how different you look compared to the last time I saw you wearing something other than your uniform. That's all."

"Oh, I guess you're right. Probably because I was trying to wear more mature clothes then."

"Really? Huh."

"Although I did buy this entire outfit only yesterday. You could call it a way of celebrating my full recovery for the time being."

"Your full recovery…"

Hitagi Senjogahara.

A girl in my class.

She had a problem until very recently. And until that very recent point in time—she'd had this problem her entire high school life.

For over two years.

Constantly.

This problem kept her from making friends, from coming in contact with anyone—it practically kept her locked inside a cage and forced her to spend a tortuous life as a high schooler—but fortunately, her problem was resolved, more or less, around last Monday. I ended up witnessing this resolution—and that was the first time I'd had a proper conversation with her, despite the two of us sharing a classroom our first, second, and now third and final years of high school. You could say it was the moment when a bond was formed between me and her, who until that point I'd seen as nothing more than a silent, delicate, illness-prone student who got good grades.

Her problem was resolved.

Resolved.

It of course wasn't so simple when you looked at it from her point of view, as the party who had dealt with the problem for a few years—how could it be? So she ended up taking time off from school until yesterday, a Saturday. She was apparently busy going to the hospital so they could investigate the issue, or run detailed tests on her, or whatever.

Then, yesterday came.

And she was freed—from all of that.

Apparently.

At long last.

Or conversely, after all.

Or inversely, for once.

"I suppose you could say that, but it's not as if the *root* of the problem has been fixed," she said. "I don't know yet if I should be honestly happy or not."

"Oh. The root of the problem."

That was the kind of problem she was dealing with.

Then again, most phenomena in the world we classify as "problems" are like that—the nature of most problems is that they're closed and finished matters from the beginning. What's important is the kind of interpretation you stick on to them.

It held true for Senjogahara.

And for me as well.

"It's fine. I'm the only one who has to worry about it," she said.

"Huh. Well, I guess you're right."

That's how it was.

For the both of us.

"I am right," she agreed. "I'm absolutely right. And I'm happy I at least have the intelligence needed to be capable of worry."

"…I wish you wouldn't make it sound like there's some unfortunate soul you know who doesn't even have the intelligence required to worry about something."

"You're an idiot, Araragi."

"And now you said it flat-out!"

She was completely ignoring the context, too.

The way that played out, it felt like she just wanted to call me stupid...

It'd been nearly a week since we last met, but she hadn't changed a bit.

I'd wondered if she was going to be a little less rough around the edges, but...

"I'm glad, though," Senjogahara said with a faint smile. "I'd planned on today being a test run, but my hope all along was for you to be the very first person who saw these clothes."

"...Huh?"

"Because I can wear whatever I want now that my problem's been solved. I can pick from anything, from everything out there to wear, with no restrictions at all."

"Ah...true."

She hadn't been able to wear whatever she wanted.

That had been one of Senjogahara's problems.

She was at the age when girls wanted to start dressing fashionably.

"I guess I, uh, feel very fortunate, or very honored to be the first person you wanted to show them to."

"I didn't say I wanted to show you, Araragi. I said I wanted you to see them. There's a world of difference between the two."

"Hunh..."

She said that, but on Monday, aside from her "mature clothes," she'd showed me much more... Still, I couldn't deny that her clothes, with all of the emphasis they placed on her chest, did quite a lot to attract my eyes. I didn't know what to call it, maybe good fashion sense, but it felt like a powerful magnetic force had captured me and wasn't letting go. She'd once passed herself off as always being ill, but now she seemed to be the complete opposite, almost positive. The outline of her upper body was easier to make out now that she had her hair up. Especially the area around her chest—hold on, I'm using the word "chest" a lot, aren't I... She wasn't showing that much skin...in fact, in her long sleeves and stockings, she wasn't showing much at all considering it was mid-May, but something about her was just exotic. What was it, how could I explain? Could it be that between experiencing

108

Hitagi Senjogahara's case on Monday and class president Tsubasa Hanekawa's case over Golden Week, I now had the ability to find the sight of a fully dressed woman more erotic than one in the nude or in her underwear?

Oh no…

That wasn't a skill I needed, not when I was only in high school…

Though to take a cooler-headed approach, it was rude for me to look at my classmates in that kind of way, plain and simple. I started to feel intense shame.

"By the way, Araragi. What exactly are you doing here in the first place? Could you have gotten yourself expelled from school during my time away? And now you're pretending to go to school while really killing time at the park because you can't bring yourself to tell your family… That would mean my worst fears have come true."

"You're making me sound like some dad who got laid off."

And today was Sunday, anyway.

Mother's Day, remember?

Just as I was on the verge of telling her this, I stopped. Senjogahara lived alone with her father due to her circumstances. Her relationship with her mother was a bit of a complicated one. It wouldn't be good to be overly sensitive to that fact, either, but it still wasn't a topic I should be bringing up for no good reason. I decided to mark the phrase "Mother's Day" as off-limits while Senjogahara was around.

And me too—

I didn't want to be talking about that either.

"Nothing, really. Just passing the time," I said.

"I once heard it said any man who answers 'just passing the time' when asked what he's doing is as good as useless. I do hope that's not true for you, though, Araragi."

"…I'm doing a little bit of bike touring."

And I mean on a bicycle, not a motorcycle, I added.

Senjogahara replied to this with a "Huh" and a nod before looking back around to the entrance of the park. Yes, where the bike parking was.

"So that bicycle was yours, Araragi?"

"Mm? Yeah."

"It was so rusted I was wondering if you had an iron oxide-plated frame, its chain had snapped and fallen, and the seat and front tire were missing. I never knew that bicycles could move in that kind of condition."

"Not that one!"

Those were the abandoned bikes.

"Didn't you notice the cool one right next to those two?! The red one! That's mine!"

"Hm... Oh. That mountain bike."

"Exactly."

"MTB."

"Uhh...I guess."

"MIB."

"That's something different."

"Hmph. So that was yours. That's odd, though. It doesn't look anything like the one you took me around on earlier."

"That's what I use to get to school. You think I'd ride a granny bike on the weekends?"

"I see, of course. You're in high school, after all, Araragi."

Senjogahara nodded. I hoped she knew that applied to her as well.

"High schooler, mountain bike," she said.

"I don't know if I like that tone of voice..."

"High schooler, mountain bike. Middle schooler, butterfly knife. Grade schooler, flipping skirts."

"And what exactly is that ominous list supposed to mean?!"

"How do you know if it's ominous or not? It was just a simple list, not any sort of sentence. You shouldn't yell at a girl based on your own assumptions, Araragi. Intimidation is like a form of assault, you know?"

In that case, so were her insults.

But there wouldn't be any point in telling her that...

"Fine, then turn that list into full sentences," I demanded.

"A high schooler with a mountain bike is like a middle schooler with a butterfly knife or a grade schooler who enjoys flipping skirts. Only more juvenile."

110

"So I was right after all!"

"Really, Araragi? That's not the quip you're supposed to make here, you're supposed to say that I'd used a sentence and a sentence fragment instead of full sentences like you'd told me."

"Do you really expect me to figure that out on the spot?!"

She didn't have some of the best grades in class for nothing.

Or maybe I was the only one in my class who wouldn't have noticed that immediately...

Language arts wasn't my strong suit.

"Hey, forget about me," I told her. "I don't even like mountain bikes that much. And I've managed to build up a bit of a tolerance to all your verbal abuse after all this time, or maybe you could say I've learned to accommodate it, but anyway, there's like, a million high schoolers around the world who ride mountain bikes. Do you really want to make enemies out of all of them?"

"Mountain bikes are incredible, aren't they? Fine articles that any high school student would naturally desire," Hitagi Senjogahara said, flip-flopping in the blink of an eye.

It seemed she was more interested in self-preservation than I'd originally thought.

"So incredible that the degree to which they don't suit you, Araragi, caused words that I in no way intended to slip out of my mouth."

"And now you're blaming me..."

"Stop nitpicking every little thing. If you're so desperate to rush to your death, I'd be happy to bring you halfway there whenever you want."

"That's as cruel as it gets!"

"Do you come around here often, Araragi?"

"You don't even hesitate to change the subject, do you? No, this is probably my first time here. I was riding around at random and happened to find a park, so I figured I'd take a break here, that's all."

To be honest, I thought I had made it much farther—maybe to the tip of Okinawa or so, but if I was running into Senjogahara, that (obviously) meant my bike hadn't even managed to get me out of town. It was like I was an animal on a farm.

Aw, dammit.

Getting a drivers license started to seem appealing.

Nah, probably after I graduate.

"What about you, Senjogahara? You said something about today being a test drive? So, what, does that mean you're walking around for physical therapy?"

"The test drive remark was referring to my clothes. Do you not do that kind of thing, Araragi, being a boy? You must at least with your shoes, don't you? But to put it simply, yes, I'm walking around."

"Huh."

"This part of town used to be my home turf."

"........."

Did she just say "turf"?

"Oh, that's right," I recalled. "You moved when you were a junior, didn't you. So you lived in this area until then or something?"

"Yes, you could say that."

So that was it.

Now it made sense—in other words, this wasn't simply about taking a walk or trying on clothes. Essentially, this was also about her feeling nostalgic for the past now that her issue had been resolved. Even Senjogahara acted like a human being now and then.

"It's been a while, but this area—" she began.

"What? It hasn't changed at all?"

"No, the opposite. It's completely different," she shot back. She must have already done a good bit of exploring. "It's not like this place is going to get me sentimental, but—it's hard to explain, it drains your motivation when you see that a town you grew up in has changed."

"It's not like you can expect it to stay the same."

I've lived in the same place ever since I was born, so to be honest, I didn't understand the feeling Senjogahara described at all. I didn't have a place I could call my country home, either...

"You're right. You can't."

Senjogahara didn't argue with me, to my surprise. It was rare for her to not come back with one opinion or another. Or maybe she thought she had nothing to gain from discussing the topic with me.

"Hey. Araragi? Do you mind if I sit next to you, then?"

"Next to me?"

"I want to talk to you."

"......"

She was always so direct about things like this.

If there was something she wanted to say or do, she stated it out-right.

Right there, out in the open.

"Sure," I said. "I was just starting to feel a little guilty about monop-olizing this four-person bench."

"Oh? Then I think I'll take a seat," Senjogahara said before sitting next to me.

She sat right next to me, so close our shoulders nearly touched.

"..............."

Um... Why was she sitting on this four-person bench like it was made for two? Aren't you a little close, Miss Senjogahara? She was so close that while, sure, our bodies weren't actually in contact, they would be with the slightest fidget. It was impressive how close she was cutting it to that line, and it seemed a little much for two classmates, or even two friends. Still, if I tried to put some distance between us, it might give the impression that I was fleeing from her. I found it hard to move when I thought about the persecution that would be brought upon me if Senjogahara happened to see it that way, even if I didn't mean it that way. The result? I froze.

"About the other day."

In this situation, in our relative positions.

Senjogahara continued to speak in a calm tone.

"I wanted to thank you for everything one more time."

"...Oh. Don't worry, there's no need to thank me, really. I didn't do a thing when you think about it."

"You're right. A piece of trash would've been more useful."

"......"

Her sentence meant the same thing as mine, but it was the meaner. What an awful woman.

"Then you should thank Oshino," I told her. "That's all you need to do."

"Mister Oshino is a separate matter. And anyway, we agreed that I'd be paying him a set fee. A hundred thousand yen, I think?"

"Yeah. So you're going to start working part-time?"

"Yes. But someone with my personality isn't fit for labor, so I'm still coming up with a plan."

"Well, at least you realize that."

"There must be some way I can skip out on this bill…"

"So what's what you meant by a plan."

"I'm joking. I'll pay my fair share. But like I said—Mister Oshino is a separate matter. I wanted to thank you in a different sense, Araragi."

"If that's the case, then you've already said enough. Even words of gratitude start to feel hollow once they're repeated too many times."

"What do you mean? They were empty from the beginning."

"They were?!"

"I'm joking. They weren't empty."

"Joking all the time, aren't you?"

I was just appalled.

Senjogahara let out a small cough.

"I'm sorry. For some reason, I always want to deny or contradict every little thing you say."

"………"

As far as apologies went, that was a hard one to accept…

It was like she was telling me that she couldn't bring herself to get along with me.

"I think I know what it is," she mused. "It's probably the same attitude that little children have of wanting to bully someone they like."

"Are you sure it isn't more like the attitude that big grownups have of wanting to torment someone they see as weak?"

Wait.

Did she just say she liked me?

No, she was just making a comparison.

It seemed pointless to adopt the middle-school mindset that every girl who smiles at you is in love with you (Smiles Are Free!), so I brought our conversation back on track.

"Really, though, I don't feel like I did anything deserving of your gratitude, and to borrow a phrase from Oshino, 'You just get saved on your own.' You don't need to bother with gratitude and that kind of thing. It'll only make it harder for us to get along from here on out."

"To get along," Senjogahara echoed without changing her tone one bit. "I—Araragi? Is it all right for me to think of us as close?"

"Of course it is."

Each of us had revealed our own problems. We weren't strangers any longer, nor simple classmates.

"Yes…yes, you're right," she said. "Each of us has the other's weakness in our hands."

"What? Is our relationship that tense?" She made it sound like it'd be strained. "It's not about weaknesses or anything, think of it as feeling close and being able to take it for granted. If you can look at it that way, I will too."

"But you're not really the type to make friends, are you, Araragi?"

"Until last year, yeah. And it wasn't my 'type' as much as it was my rule. But I had a bit of a paradigm shift over spring break, and, well… What about you, Senjogahara?"

"That was me until last Monday," she said. "To elaborate, it was until I met you, Araragi."

"………"

What was with this girl…

Actually, what was with this situation…

It practically felt like she was confessing her love to me. The air felt heavy, even stifling…like I hadn't had time to prepare myself emotionally for the moment. I would've paid more attention to my clothes and my hair if I knew this would be coming, and…

Wait, no!

I was feeling embarrassed for putting honest thought into how I should react if she started telling me she loved me! And why were my eyes getting drawn to Senjogahara's chest as soon as I started thinking about that?! Was I that trite of a person?! Was Koyomi Araragi the kind of classless, vulgar man who judged a girl on the basis of her (chest's) appearance—

"What's wrong, Araragi?"

"Oh, um…I'm sorry."

"Why are you apologizing?"

"I'm starting to think my very existence is a crime…"

"Uh huh. You ought to be illegal."

"………"

Hold on.

Again, she was repeating what I said but with a completely different nuance.

"Anyway, Araragi," she said. "Regardless of what you say, I want to pay you back. Because if I don't, I'll always feel like you have something on me. If we want to become friends, I think we only can after I pay you back first. That way we can be friends on an equal footing."

"Friends…"

Friends.

What could it have been?

I knew it was supposed to be an emotional, touching word, but it felt like a part of me was disappointed to hear it, like I was feeling despondent after putting too many expectations on it…

No, that wasn't it…

That wasn't it at all…

"What's the matter, Araragi? I thought that was a pretty good speech just now, but you look let down for some reason."

"No, no, I'm not. It just looks that way because I'm doing everything I can to hide how I really feel. Hearing you say that makes me so excited I could do the can-can."

"I see."

She gave one of those unconvinced nods.

She might have even thought that I had some kind of ulterior motive.

"Well, in any case—Araragi. Is there anything you want me to do for you? Whatever you want, just this one time."

"…A-Anything?"

"Anything."

"Oh…"

A girl in my class had just told me that she'd do anything I asked her to do...

It suddenly felt like I had accomplished something truly great.

....

But she had to know what she was doing.

"Anything, really," she assured. "Any one wish you have, I'll grant. Whether that's world domination, eternal life, or to defeat the Saiyans on their way to this Earth."

"Are you telling me that you're more powerful than Shenlong?!"

"Of course I am."

She said yes?!

"But don't lump me in with a traitor who becomes your enemy in the end after being useless when it matters the most... Really, though, I'd prefer to be asked to grant wishes that are more personal. Those are easier, after all."

"I'd imagine so..."

"But it looks like you're having trouble coming up with something after being put on the spot like this, Araragi? In that case, we could always go with, well, you know. The standard wish in this kind of situation. Where for your one wish you ask for a hundred wishes or something."

"...Huh? Wait, is that allowed here?"

That was one of the most standard taboos in this kind of situation. I'd have to be shameless to even attempt that one.

And she said it herself.

That'd be like pledging her obedience to me.

"Please, whatever you want. I'll do my best to make it happen. There must be lots of things that appeal to you, like me ending all my sentences with '-mew' for a week, or me going to school with no underwear on for a week, or me coming to wake you up every morning in nothing but an apron for a week, or me helping you use enemas to go on a diet for a week."

"Is that the kind of pervert you think I am?! That's just rude!"

"Well...um, I'm sorry, but I don't think I could bring myself to do any of those for the rest of my life..."

"No! No, no, no! I'm not mad at you because you thought I was less of a freak than I am, it's the opposite!"

"Is that so?" Senjogahara said primly.

She was clearly toying with me...

"And wait, Senjogahara. Are you saying you'd actually go along with any of those if it was for a week?"

"I'm prepared to, yes."

".........."

Well, you don't need to be, I thought.

"For your reference, my personal recommendation would be the apron for a week. Not only am I a morning person, I'm already getting up early every day, so I'm even willing to make breakfast for you while I'm at it. Still in nothing but an apron, of course. Isn't watching a girl do that from the back one of the great male fantasies?"

"Hey, don't talk about 'male fantasies' like that! They're all way cooler! Plus, if you did that at my home when people were around it would tear my family apart faster than you could say gale-force winds!"

"You make it sound like it wouldn't be a problem if your family isn't around. All right then, would you like to stay at my home for a week? I assume the end result would be the same, though."

"Listen, Senjogahara," I said, this time in a stern voice. "Even if we somehow came to an agreement like that, I don't think it'd be possible for us to keep being friends afterwards."

"Oh. Now that you mention it, you're right. Yes, of course. In that case, nothing erotic."

Of course not.

And wait, so Senjogahara saw ending all of her sentences with "-mew" as an erotic request... She had some pretty out-there interests despite her cool demeanor.

"I know you would never ask me for something erotic, anyway," she said.

"Oh. You really trust me, don't you?"

"You're a virgin, after all."

".........."

I guess I had told her that.

118

Just last week, in fact.

"It's nice and easy being with a virgin. They never ask for much."

"Um… Wait a second, Senjogahara. You've been saying stuff about virgins since the other time, but it's not like you have any experience yourself, do you? So it's hard to appreciate anything you say regarding the topic—"

"What are you talking about? I do have experience."

"You do?"

"I do it all over the place," Senjogahara let slip casually.

All she cared about was contradicting every single thing I said, it seemed…

And "all over the place"? Really?

"Uhh, I don't know how I should respond to that, but even if, hypothetically, that were somehow true, what could you possibly gain out of telling me that fact, Senjogahara?"

"…Hrm," she murmured.

Not without blushing.

I was the one doing the blushing, though, not her.

This conversation was reaching a lot of limits.

"All right, fine… Allow me to make a correction," Senjogahara finally said. "I don't have any experience. I'm a virgin."

"…Okay."

She was confessing to me, but not in the way I'd imagined at all.

Though she did force me to say the same thing the other day, so technically speaking, we were even now.

"In other words!" Senjogahara then thrust her index finger toward me and began yelling in a voice that might have carried throughout the park, "The only kind of girl who would ever talk to a lame, virgin loser like you is a crazy spinster like me!"

"…!"

So… So she was even prepared to degrade herself if it meant more verbal abuse to hurl at me…

I didn't know which I wanted to do more, take my hat off to her or wave a white flag at her.

I was prepared to surrender unconditionally.

Of course, there was no need for me to dig too deep into this subject after learning about Senjogahara's fixation on chastity in a traumatizing manner the week before. With her, it wasn't a personality issue but something of a condition.

"We've gotten off track," I said.

Senjogahara began speaking to me in a composed voice again. "Really, isn't there something, Araragi? Something that's bothering you on a simple level, maybe."

"Something that's bothering me, huh?"

"I'm not very good with words so this is hard for me to say well, but I really do want to help you."

I wasn't so sure about the "not very good with words" part.

If anything, she was too good with them, and that was her problem—but still, Hitagi Senjogahara.

She wasn't a bad person—at the root.

So even if it hadn't been banned...

I'd have a tough time tossing any kind of immodest request her way.

"For example," she offered, "maybe you want me to teach you how to overcome being a shut-in."

"How could I possibly be a shut-in? In what world would a shut-in own a mountain bike?"

"You never know, there might be one. I won't let you discriminate against shut-ins like that, Araragi. They probably take the tires off then pedal away inside their room or something."

"That'd be an exercise bike."

What a healthy shut-in that would be.

But yeah, maybe they did exist.

"Either way, it's hard to come up with something that's bothering me on the spot."

"Yes, I can see that. You don't have any bed head today, after all."

"Are you saying that the only problems I have to deal with are things like having messy hair?!"

"Where are you getting all of that from? I never knew you had such a strong persecution complex. You read between the lines too much, Araragi, you know that?"

"What else could you have meant by it?"

Sheesh.

She was like a rose whose petals were made out of thorns, too.

"I should be able to help you with other problems, like if there's a girl in your class who's nice to everyone except for you."

"Next subject!"

It felt like the conversation would go on like this forever unless I forced myself to come up with something.

Agh...

Seriously.

"Something that's bothering me, you say... Well, if I had to come up with something, it might not exactly qualify as bothering me, but—"

"Oh, so you do have something."

"Sure, of course I do."

"What could it be? Tell me."

"You really go straight for it, don't you?"

"Of course. This is the moment of truth when I learn whether or not I can pay you back, Araragi. Or is this something that's awkward to talk about?"

"No, not really."

"Then let me hear it. Just talking about it will make you feel better—or so they say."

......

I don't know, it wasn't convincing coming from someone who used to be as secretive as her.

"Umm... I got in a fight with my siblings."

"...I'm a little doubtful I can help you with that."

So quick to give up.

She hadn't even heard the details, either...

"But go ahead," she said, "you might as well tell me the whole story."

"I might as well?"

"Okay, tell me the whole story, for the time being."

"Was that rephrasing even worth it?"

"Time's a-wasting, then."

"...Well, uh, sure."

I'd just told myself the words were off-limits, but…

I had to use them, given where the conversation had taken us.

"Today's Mother's Day, right?" I asked.

"Huh? Oh, I suppose it is, now that you mention it," Senjogahara replied normally.

I guess I was being overly sensitive after all.

Which meant all that was left—was my own problem.

"So, which of your siblings did you fight with? You have two little sisters, right?"

"Right, I guess you knew. If I had to say just one, it'd be the older of the two—but I basically fought with both of them. They're inseparable wherever they are or whatever they're up to, the Five W's."

"They are Tsuganoki Second Middle School's famed Fire Sisters, after all."

"You know them by their alias?"

Something about that bothered me.

Not as much as the fact that my sisters had an alias, though.

"Both of them are tight with our mother, too—and she treats the two of them like her favorite little pets. So—"

"I see," Senjogahara cut me off as if she now understood the situation. She all but told me that I didn't need to finish my thought. "So you, the oldest son of the family, feel like there's no place for you at home today on Mother's Day, being the failure that you are."

"…That's right."

While Senjogahara probably considered the "failure" remark to be on a continuum with her standard arsenal of verbal abuse, it was unfortunately the unexaggerated, stark truth. I had no choice but to agree.

It was a stretch to say there was no place for me at home.

But I wouldn't have said there's no place like home, either.

"And that's why you've toured your way up here. Hmph. I don't understand, though. Why would that cause you to get in a fight with your sisters?"

"I tried to sneak out of the house early this morning, but my sisters caught me as I was trying to get on my mountain bike. Then we had an argument."

"An argument?"

"They wanted me to spend Mother's Day together with everyone—but it feels like, you know, I can't do that kind of thing."

"You know, you say. I can't, you say," Senjogahara repeated meaningfully.

Maybe she was trying to tell me something.

Like, what a nice problem to have.

Senjogahara lived alone with her father—so it would be, from her perspective.

"A lot of us girls start to hate our fathers around middle school—are boys the same way with their mothers?"

"Eh… It's not that I don't like her, or that I hate her, it just feels awkward around her, and well, when I'm around my sisters, I more or less feel the same way, and—"

—You know, Koyomi, that's why.

—That's why you'll never—

"…But you see, Senjogahara, that's not the problem here. Not having fought with my sisters, not Mother's Day, it's not the specifics that are bothering me—this stuff tends to happen on any kind of special day. It's just…"

"It's just what?"

"What I'm trying to say is that regardless of the circumstances, I'm not able to bring myself to celebrate Mother's Day, and I'm getting honestly upset at something that my sister who's four years younger than me said, and, I don't know, I'm just so annoyed at how petty of a person I am that I can't take it."

"Huh—what a complicated problem to have," Senjogahara said. "You've gone all the way around and turned it into a meta-problem. Like which came first, the chicken or the chick."

"The chick, of course."

"Is that so."

"It's not a complicated problem, it's a paltry one, that's all. Woe is me, I'm a petty person. But still, I really don't want to go home when I think about how I'm going to have to apologize to my little sister. I almost want to live here in this park for the rest of my life."

"You don't want to go home, huh?"

Senjogahara sighed.

"Unfortunately, fixing your pettiness is beyond my abilities…"

"…Can't you at least try?"

"Clearly, fixing your pettiness is beyond my abilities…"

"…"

Even if it was clear, it only further depressed me to hear her put it in such a succinct and crestfallen manner. Of course, this wasn't serious enough to get depressed about, but precisely the degree to which it wasn't serious made me feel uncomfortably small.

"I feel like I'm such a lame person. If I had to have worries, I wish they could at least be about world peace or how to bring happiness to all of humanity. But instead, my worries are this small-minded thing. That's—what I can't stand."

"Small-minded—"

"Maybe 'pathetic' would be a better word. The way it'd feel if every time you got a scratch-off lottery ticket, all you ever won was another free ticket."

"You shouldn't degrade what makes you so charming, Araragi."

"Charming?! My charm is the ability to win free lottery tickets?!"

"I'm joking. And when I think of how pathetic you are, that isn't how I would describe it."

"I'd never win anything, no matter how many tickets I bought?"

"Are you kidding me? That'd be impressive in its own way. When I think of how pathetic you are, Araragi…"

Senjogahara made sure to wait a few moments in order to give extra weight to what she was about to say.

"It's the kind of pathetic that would win the jackpot and tell all his friends about it, only to realize later that it's a nominal sum."

I slowly chewed on and digested the words.

"God, that's pathetic!" I screamed.

That was as pathetic as you could get…and she'd come up with that on the spot. A frightening woman, as always—more than ever, really.

"Putting aside the stuff with your mother for now, the fighting with your sister part does seem petty. I would have thought you were the kind of brother who doted on his little sisters."

"All we ever do is fight," I said.

And today—today was especially bad.

Because it wasn't a weekday.

"So instead of finding them cute, they make you cringe?"

"There's nothing cringe-worthy about my sisters!"

"Or could this be the flip side of love? Do you have a thing for your sisters, Araragi?"

"No. The idea of being in love with your little sister is a delusion held by people who don't actually have little sisters. That would never happen in real life."

"Wow, Araragi. It's very ugly of you to act superior just because they don't have something you do."

....

What was she even trying to say?

"You know, like, 'Oh, money's not important,' or 'I wish I'd never gotten a girlfriend!' or 'What school you went to doesn't matter'... Don't you hate those kinds of arrogant people?"

"Having a little sister is a bit different from those examples..."

"I see. So you're not romantically interested in your little sisters? You'd never fall in love with them?"

"How could I?"

"Right, I guess you do strike me as more of a sororate fetishist."

Sororate?

That was a word I hadn't heard before.

"You know, like a sororate marriage? Levirate marriage for women, where a man's wife dies, so he marries her sister."

"...I'm as amazed as ever by your vast wealth of knowledge, but why would I be a soro-whatever?"

"You have younger sisters, not older sisters. I bet you'll have a girl who's unrelated to you call you 'big brother,' as her brother-in-law, before you marry her...and make her call you 'big brother' even after you're husband and wife. Now that's a true, realistic representation of—"

"I bet I also murdered my original wife!" I reacted to Senjogahara's words before she could finish, a violation of traditional straight-man etiquette.

"Anyway, you sororate fetishist—"

"Just call me a sister-lover, please!"

"You said you'd never fall in love with your biological sisters."

"I didn't say I would if it were my sister-in-law!"

"So you'll be falling in love with a girlfriend-in-law."

"Again…wait, what? You can have a girlfriend-in-law?"

What the hell.

When I gave it a bit more thought, it made some sort of sense. But in that case, what might a biological girlfriend… No, I was getting way off track…

"You really are a small-minded person if you get worked up by a few minor remarks like that," Senjogahara said.

"Your remarks are anything but minor."

"I was only testing you."

"Why are you testing me? And wait, does that mean you're holding back?!"

"If I gave it my all, I'd transform."

"Transform?! Whoa, now that, I wanna see!"

Well, part of me did, but part of me didn't…

Senjogahara exhaled and looked pensive.

"You're a very small person for how big your reactions are. I wonder if there's some kind of relation. But I won't give up on you, Araragi, no matter how small you are. I promise to be right there by your side, every petty step you take."

"You and your subtle jabs."

"I'll always be by your side. From the mountains in the west to the oceans of the east. Even down into hell, if I must."

"…You see, that line might cast you in a good light, but what does it say about me?"

"So is there anything bothering you that doesn't involve your pettiness?"

"………"

Did she hate me or what?

Was I a victim of some severe bullying here?

126

I was beginning to hope that I just had a persecution complex.

"There's nothing in particular…" I said.

"And there's nothing you desire, either—hmm…"

"I wonder what kind of abuse you'll be hurling at me next."

"It's fabulous how much of a broad-minded, accepting person you are."

"False praise if I've ever heard any!"

"It's fantabulous, Araragi."

"Like I just said… What was that? Some sort of soda ad?"

"It's a combination of 'fantastic' and 'fabulous.' Have you really never heard that before?"

"No…and you must be up to something to go so far as to pull out a neologism that must have died generations ago to praise me."

And of all the things to say, "broad-minded"…when I was just telling her about how petty I was.

"I just thought I'd strike first. I was afraid you'd tell me 'no insults for a week' or something."

"Like you'd really be able to do that," I scoffed.

It'd be tantamount to asking her to stop breathing, or for her heart to stop beating.

And if you took insults away from Senjogahara, even for a week, she wouldn't be Senjogahara. It wouldn't be any fun for me, either… Hold on, since when did I turn into the kind of character that relied on Senjogahara's abuse to keep going?

This was getting dangerous…

"Fine, then… Though it was shocking to see you without a single idea the moment I banned erotic requests."

"That may be true, but I didn't have any ideas before you banned them either."

"Okay, Araragi, I get it. Then I'll allow them, as long as they're only mildly sexual. Upon my name, I hereby allow you to unleash your desires."

"………"

Did she actually want me to?

Great, now I was feeling overly self-conscious. This was getting dizzying.

"Do you really not have anything? You don't want me to help you with your homework?"

"I've given up on that already. Just as long as I can graduate."

"Then how about being able to graduate?"

"I'll do that fine if I just proceed normally!"

"Then how about just being able to proceed normally?"

"You're picking a fight with me, aren't you, aren't you?!"

"Then how about, say—"

Senjogahara made a show of waiting a measured pause, of getting her timing right, before continuing.

"Having a girlfriend?"

"………"

Was this—another case of being too self-conscious?

It seemed to be a meaningful statement.

"And what would happen…if I said yes?"

"You'd get a girlfriend," she coolly replied. "That's all."

I sat there in silence.

Yeah…

If you felt like it, it was definitely the kind of line you could read into.

To be honest, I had no clue what kind of situation I had gotten myself in—but it seemed wrong to take advantage of someone who's in your gratitude, regardless of what happened and how. Forget about ethics and morals, it simply didn't feel right.

A girlfriend-in-law—was it?

What Oshino said was starting to make sense.

You just got saved on your own.

From Oshino's perspective, what I'd done—for Senjogahara, for the class president, and for that woman over spring break…for the demon—may have been beautiful, but it wasn't right.

No one else solved Senjogahara's problems, her own sincere thinking did.

In that sense—it would be uncouth.

No matter what I asked for.

So.

"No, nothing like that either, really," I said.

"Hmph. I see."

Even if there was some deeper meaning hidden in what she'd said, it turned unknowable once more, whatever it may have been—as Senjogahara spoke those emotionless words.

"Buy me a soda next time or something, and we'll call it even."

"I see. A stranger to greed."

You really are broad-minded, she said, as if to tie in everything.

It must have been her way of signaling that she was done with the topic.

So.

I decided to face forward. It felt like I had been looking at Senjogahara's face for a long while, so I focused on something else, whether intentionally or out of awkwardness—and there.

And there I saw a girl.

A girl carrying a large backpack.

003

The girl looked to be in late elementary school, and she was heading toward a metal sign at the edge of the park—a residential map of the area. Her back was to me, so I had no idea what she looked like, but the large backpack she carried was just so notable—which meant I recognized her immediately. That's right, she was facing that residential map in the same way only moments earlier, before Senjogahara showed up. It didn't take long for her to run off that time—but she seemed to have returned. From the looks of it, she was comparing a note she carried with what was printed on the sign.

Hmm.

In other words, she was a lost child. The note must have had a handwritten map or an address written on it.

I focused my sight on her.

And when I did, I noticed a nametag sewn onto her backpack—"Grade 5, Class 3," and her name inscribed with a thick permanent marker.

I wasn't a hundred percent sure how you read the characters for her first name, but…it was probably "Mayoi."

Her last name, though… How was it read? I'd never seen it before. "Yakudera"…maybe?

Language arts wasn't my strong suit.

In that case, I thought, I'd try asking someone for whom it was.

"…Hey, Senjogahara. You see that grade schooler in front of that sign? How do you read that last name written on her backpack?"

"Huh?" Senjogahara looked puzzled. "Are you kidding me? I can't even see it."

"Oh…"

Right.

I'd forgotten.

My body wasn't normal anymore—and I'd *fed* Shinobu my blood the day before, on Saturday. At that moment, my physical abilities were far greater than normal, though not to the degree they had been over spring break. That of course went for my vision, too. If I wasn't careful—I'd see things in the far distance like they were right in front of me. It's not as if making them out posed a problem, but seeing stuff that other people don't—isn't such a good feeling.

It creates discord with others.

Senjogahara had that problem, too.

"Umm…" I said to her, "it's written with the characters for the numbers eight and nine, followed by the one for 'temple'…"

"…? Well, you'd read that as 'Hachikuji.'"

"'Hachikuji'?"

"Yes. Are you that illiterate, Araragi? At your academic level, I'm surprised you managed to graduate kindergarten."

"I could graduate kindergarten with my eyes closed!"

"That is a gross overestimation of your own abilities."

"Now you're even nitpicking my retorts?!"

"You're not going to impress anyone with those kinds of conceited remarks."

"You're impressing me, for what it's worth…"

"But seriously, anyone with so much as a slight interest in Japanese history or classics, which is to say anyone with any intellectual curiosity, would know how to read it. There are such things as dumb questions, Araragi, and you're dumb whether or not you ask them."

"Yeah, okay, whatever. I'm a bad student."

"You're sorely mistaken if you think recognizing that fact makes it any better."

"……"

Had I done something to her?

I could have sworn we were just talking about how she was going to thank me…

"Sheesh… Well, anyway," I said. "So I guess that means her name is read 'Mayoi Hachikuji.'"

What an odd name.

Then again, it might have been more normal than "Hitagi Senjogahara" or "Koyomi Araragi." Whatever the case, it wasn't in good taste to go on about people's names.

"Um…" I began, looking toward Senjogahara.

Hmph.

I couldn't imagine her being the type to like little kids… She seemed more the type to toss a ball in the opposite direction if one came rolling her way. I could see her punting a crying child for being too loud.

Which meant that it'd be safest to go alone.

If it were anyone other than Senjogahara, I'd want to bring a girl with me so the child might lower her guard.

But that was off the table.

"Hey, could you wait here for a minute?"

"That's fine with me, but where are you off to?"

"I'm going to talk to that elementary school kid."

"I wouldn't if I were you. You'll only end up feeling hurt."

"………"

She really didn't think twice before saying some awful things, did she?

Whatever, we could discuss that later.

For now, that child.

Mayoi Hachikuji.

I stood up from the bench and jogged across the park—to where the metal sign stood, where the girl with the backpack was. She seemed engrossed in comparing the map to her note and didn't notice me approaching her from behind.

I called to her when only a step remained between us.

I tried to sound as friendly and sociable as I could.

"Hey there. What's the matter, are you lost?"

The girl turned around.

She wore her hair in pigtails, with bangs so short her eyebrows were showing.

Her face gave me the impression that she was bright.

The girl—Mayoi Hachikuji—scrutinized me first before opening her mouth.

"Please don't speak to me. I don't like you."

"………"

………

I returned to the bench in a zombie-like gait.

Senjogahara looked at me quizzically.

"What's the matter? Did something happen?"

"I'm feeling hurt… I only ended up feeling hurt…"

The damage was even worse than I expected.

It took a dozen or so seconds for me to recover.

"…I'm going again."

"And where are you off to, and why?"

"Can't you tell just from watching?"

With that, I tried anew.

The girl, Hachikuji, had returned to looking at the sign as if her encounter with me had never taken place. She was checking it against her note. I took a peek at it from over her shoulder—and on it was an address, not a map. I wasn't sure, not knowing the area, but it had to be nearby.

"Hey, you."

"………"

"You're lost, right? Where do you want to go?"

"………"

"Here, let me look at that note."

"………"

"………"

………

I returned to the bench in a zombie-like gait.

"What's the matter? Did something happen?"

134

"I got ignored… I was given the silent treatment by an elementary school girl…"

The damage was even worse than I expected.

It took a dozen or so seconds for me to recover.

"This time will be different… I'm going."

"You know, Araragi, I don't really understand what it is you're trying to do, or why you're doing it…"

"Just leave me alone…"

With that, I tried for the third time.

The girl, Hachikuji, was facing the sign.

Figuring that the first to act had the advantage, I smacked her in the back of the head. Her guard all the way down, Hachikuji's exposed forehead bumped into the sign.

"Wh-What are you doing?!"

She did turn around.

Thank goodness.

"Anyone would turn around after being smacked from behind!" she accused.

"Er…I'm sorry for smacking you." All of those repeated shocks to my system had caused me to lose my cool. "Life is full of pain, you know?"

"I'm not seeing your point!"

"It shines brightest when…you know?"

"I was seeing stars just now!"

"Yup…"

I wasn't fooling her.

Too bad.

"Well, you seem like you're having some trouble. I thought I might be able to help out."

"There's no help in this world that someone who sneaks up on grade schoolers and smacks them in the head could possibly give! Absolutely, positively none!"

Her guard was up. Way up.

Of course it was.

"Like I said, I'm sorry. Really, I apologize. Um, my name is Koyomi

Araragi."

"Koyomi? That's a girly name."

"………"

She didn't hold back, did she.

I rarely ever got that from people I was meeting for the first time.

"You reek of girlishness!" she exclaimed. "Please don't come near me!"

"I'm not going to stand for a woman saying that to me, even if she is in elementary school…"

Whoa, there.

Calm down, calm down.

You have to start—with trust.

We wouldn't be getting anywhere unless I tried to ameliorate the situation.

"So, what's your name?" I asked her.

"I'm Mayoi Hachikuji. I'm called Mayoi Hachikuji. My name is a precious gift from my father and mother."

"Huh…"

It seemed we were right about how the name was read.

"Anyway, please don't speak to me! I don't like you!"

"Why not?"

"Because you suddenly smacked me from behind."

"But you said you didn't like me even before I smacked you."

"Then it's karma from a previous life!"

"My first time being disliked in such a way."

"You and I were mortal enemies in our past lives! I was a lovely princess and you were the evil demon king!"

"You're just kidnapping yourself here, let's be clear."

Don't follow strangers.

If a stranger talks to you, ignore him.

Elementary school students in this day and age probably have that lesson pounded into them… Or is it just that my appearance is unappealing to kids?

Whichever the case, not being liked by a child is a real downer.

"Just calm down for a second," I said. "I'm not going to harm you

136

or anything. I'm known as a 'friend to man and beast alike' in this town, okay?"

That was definitely a stretch, but it seemed like the right degree of exaggeration considering who I was dealing with. Child or not, it's smart to make yourself appear as innocuous as possible to cases like her.

Whether or not she was convinced, she gave a solemn nod and said, "I understand. I'll lower my guard."

"I'd appreciate that."

"Okay then, Mister Beast Alike."

"Mister Beast Alike?! Are you talking about me?!"

Ack…

It was a common set phrase, but you could twist it into a supremely condescending insult simply by setting off the last part. What an expression for me to have been using thoughtlessly. In fact, I hadn't just used it, but presented myself as such…

…

"You're yelling at me! You're scary!" she said.

"Okay, I'm sorry I yelled, but you shouldn't go around calling people 'Mister Beast Alike'! That'd make anyone start yelling!"

"Really… But you said yourself that you're known as it. All I did was respond in a sincere manner."

"You can't go around assuming that you can say anything as long as you're being sincere. That's not how the world works…"

True, in this instance the words themselves came from me, and perhaps she wasn't even being critical. But still.

"In short, 'friend to man and beast alike' isn't a phrase you want to recast like that," I said.

"Oh. Is that so? I see. In other words, it's like 'Jumpin' Jehosaphat!' People may find a character who screeches out 'Jumpin' Jehosaphat!' whenever he gets excited acceptable, but they'd never buy a character 'with a tendency to call upon a leaping biblical king when agitated.' Like that?" she asked.

"I'm not so sure about that one… I don't see myself ever approving of a character who screeches out 'Jumpin' Jehosaphat!' whenever he gets excited…"

"Then how shall I refer to you?"

"Like normal."

"Okay. Mister Araragi, then."

"I like it. Normal. Can't beat normal."

"I don't like you, Mister Araragi."

"……"

My situation hadn't improved a bit.

"You reek! Please don't come near me!"

"Isn't that somehow worse than reeking of girlishness?!"

"Hrmph… You're right, 'reek' on its own may have been a very mean way to describe you. Allow me to correct myself."

"If you're really going to, then sure."

"You reek of it! Please don't come near me!"

"The first part almost made sense, but you messed it up!"

"I don't care! Please go somewhere else with due haste!"

"No, wait… You're lost, right?"

"I'm completely able to cope with this kind of situation! I'm used to problems like this! This is a very normal thing for me! I'm used to getting into travel!"

"You work in the industry on and off?! At that age?!"

If that were the case, she wouldn't get lost, would she?

"Just…stop being stubborn," I told her.

"I'm not being stubborn!"

"Yes you are."

"Hiya! Take this!"

As Hachikuji uttered the words, she unleashed a high kick in my direction that had all of her body weight behind it. Unbefitting of a grade schooler, her kick had beautiful form as if a rod ran through her spine keeping it perfectly straight. Sadly, there's something of a height gap between elementary school and high school students, and it proved insurmountable. It might have turned out differently had she caught me square in the face, but her high kick only made it up to my armpit. That isn't to say that the tip of her shoe hitting me there didn't do any damage, but the pain was bearable. Immediately after her foot hit me, I used my arms to grab her around her ankle and calf.

"Dear I!" Hachikuji cried out, but it was too late.

…Deciding to ask Senjogahara later about the grammaticality of "Dear I," for now, as Hachikuji wobbled on one leg, I yanked her up the way a farmer might jerk a large radish out of his field. If this were judo, you'd call it a hip throw. It's against the rule to grab your opponent's leg like that in judo, but unfortunately for her, this was real combat, not some match. As soon as her body left the ground, I was treated to a glimpse of the contents of her skirt, at a fairly racy angle, but not being a pedophile I wasn't distracted one bit. I simply tossed her over my shoulder.

Here, however, the gap in our heights worked against me. Thanks to her small frame, Hachikuji spent a slightly longer amount of time airborne before being slammed to the ground than a person my size—just slightly, but that was all it took for Hachikuji to change her approach and grab my hair with her free hands. I was growing it out for a reason—which meant that even Hachikuji's short fingers had no problem grabbing hold of it. Pain shot through my scalp and shocked my hand into letting go of Hachikuji's calf.

Hachikuji was not such a sweet girl as to waste this opportunity. Instead of waiting to land, she stayed on my back, pivoted around me using my shoulder blades, and began raining down blows on my head. Elbowing me. Her strikes found their mark—but were shallow. She wasn't able to convey her accustomed amount of force because her feet were off the ground. Our difference in age and experience showed. If she'd dealt a single sure blow instead of rushing the outcome, that would have been it, she could have ended it. Now it was my turn to counterattack. I had a guaranteed path to victory.

I grabbed the arm that was elbowing me in the head—it felt like the left—no, it was reversed, so her right arm—grabbed her right arm, and from that stance redid my throw!

This time—it worked.

Hachikuji's back slammed onto the ground.

I put some distance between the two of us, wary of a possible counterattack—

But she showed no signs of getting up.

I'd won.

"You fool—you thought a grade schooler could beat a high schooler! Fwahahahahaha!"

There he stood, a male high school senior, bragging in earnest about beating a grade school girl, having fought her in earnest and dispatched her with an earnest hip throw.

That high schooler would be me.

I, Koyomi Araragi, was the kind of character who bullied a grade school girl and burst into laughter... I was managing to creep myself out.

"...Araragi," a cool voice came.

I looked around to find Senjogahara.

She seemed to have come up to me because she couldn't bear watching.

Her expression was a very dubious one.

"I know I said I'd follow you down into hell, but we were talking about being small. Being cringe-worthy is something else entirely, I hope you realize."

"...Allow me to defend myself."

"Go ahead."

"........."

My actions were indefensible.

I searched in vain.

So I regrouped.

"Well, forget about what's past for now, this girl over here—" I pointed to Hachikuji, still unable to get off the ground. I assumed she'd be fine, though. She'd hit the ground back first, which meant her backpack would have cushioned the blow. "She seems to be lost. And as far as I can tell, she doesn't seem to be with a parent or a friend or anyone else. I've, um, been here in this park for a while since this morning, and she was actually here looking at this sign before you arrived. I didn't make anything of it then, but she came back, so she must really be lost, right? I wouldn't want anyone to be worrying about her, so I wondered if I could be of some help."

"...Hunh."

Although Senjogahara nodded, her expression remained dubious. Sure, I could see how she might want to ask how the situation went from that to getting into a brawl, but what could I say? It was simply a case of one warrior's soul answering another.

"I see."

"Huh?"

"No, it makes sense... Now I see what's going on."

Did she really?

Heh, maybe she was just pretending she understood.

"Oh, that's right, Senjogahara. You used to live around here, didn't you? So you'd probably know roughly where an address in the neighborhood is if you heard it?"

"Um, sure...as well as the average person."

A lukewarm answer.

Was it possible that she now considered me a child abuser? That seemed like an even worse label than pedophile, if that was possible.

"Hey, Hachikuji," I said. "I know you're only acting like you've passed out. Show the nice lady over here your note."

I crouched down and looked at Hachikuji's face.

Her eyes were rolled back.

...She really had passed out.

Seeing the whites of a little girl's eyes was pretty distressing...

"What's wrong, Araragi?"

"Oh, nothing..."

I casually turned to hide Hachikuji's face behind my back so that Senjogahara wouldn't notice and slapped the girl's cheeks a few times. This of course wasn't an additional act of violence, but an attempt to wake her up.

She came to as a result.

"Hm...I think I just had a dream."

"Oh, really? What kind of dream was that?" I said in my best public TV children's show voice. "Tell me, Hachikuji! What kind of dream did you have?"

"A dream where I was physically abused by a savage high school kid."

"…Sounds like one of those dreams where the opposite of reality happens."

"I see. So that's what it was."

It was unmistakably what had happened to her right before she passed out.

Remorse was tearing its way through my chest.

I took Hachikuji's note from her and tried to hand it to Senjogahara—but she made no attempt to take it. She stared at my outstretched hand, her eyes colder than ice.

"What's the matter? Take it."

"…I somehow just don't want to touch you."

Urg.

I thought I had gotten used to her acid tongue, but this stung…

"I'm only handing you a note."

"I don't want to touch anything that's touched you."

"……"

She hated me now…

Senjogahara straight up hated me now…

But how weird… It felt like we were getting along pretty well until just a few moments ago.

"Fine, I get it… Then I'll read it out for you, okay? Let's see…"

I read the address exactly as it was written on the note. Fortunately, I was able to do so fluently because there weren't any opaque characters.

"Ah," Senjogahara said in response. "I know where that is."

"Great."

"I guess it would be a little bit past my old home. I don't know the area in detail, but we should be able to feel it out once we're nearby. Okay, let's go."

Senjogahara turned around and began walking in long strides toward the park entrance as soon as she finished speaking. I expected her to complain more, or to say she didn't want to have to show a child around, but she was surprisingly quick to agree—then again, she didn't so much as introduce herself to Hachikuji or even make eye contact with her, so I assumed my prediction that she disliked children still held. That, or she was considering this to be my "any one wish."

142

Ah…

It'd really feel like I'd wasted my wish if that were the case…

"Well, whatever… Let's go, Hachikuji."

"What? Go where?" Hachikuji asked, seeming honestly confused.

Was she not able to pick up on conversations or something?

"To the address on this note, of course. The lady over there knows where it is, so she agreed to take us there. Isn't that great?"

"…Oh. She wants to?"

"Hm? Wait, are you not lost?"

"No, I am lost," Hachikuji affirmed. "I'm a lost snail."

"Huh? A lost snail?"

"No, I—" She shook her head. "I'm nothing."

"…Okay, then. Um, in that case, I guess we should follow after that lady. Her name's Senjogahara. And if you think her name seems aggressive, just wait until you get to know her. Once you get used to her bristliness, though, you might acquire a taste for it because on the inside, she's a fairly honest, good person. Maybe a little too honest."

"……"

"Come on. Just hurry up and follow me."

Hachikuji still wasn't moving, so I grabbed her hand and pulled, almost dragged, her with me to chase after Senjogahara. "Ah, urr, err, orkork," Hachikuji vocalized the kind of bizarre sounds you'd expect from a porpoise or a sea lion, but despite a few close calls, she followed me all the way without tripping a single time.

I'd come back later for my mountain bike.

For now, we left the park, whatever it was named. I never got a chance to figure that one out.

004

I think it's finally time to talk about my spring break.

It happened during spring break.

I was attacked by a vampire.

Though it was less an attack and more of me sticking my own neck out—as in literally thrusting it toward a pair of sharp fangs—in any case, I, Koyomi Araragi, in this day and age where science reigns supreme, where there is no darkness that cannot be illuminated, was attacked by a vampire in a backwater Japanese suburb.

By a beautiful demon.

Attacked—by a blood-chillingly gorgeous demon.

My blood was—sucked dry.

As a result, I became a vampire.

I know it sounds like a joke, but it's not an amusing one.

My body was burned by the sun, hated crosses, was weakened by garlic, and melted in holy water—and in exchange, I gained unbe-lievable physical abilities. Then, waiting for me at the very end of my saga—was a hellish reality. I was saved from that reality by a dude passing by, scratch that, Mèmè Oshino. A role model to none with no fixed address who wandered from journey to journey, Mèmè Oshino. He somehow managed to vanquish the vampire—and pulled off a bunch of other things.

And so—I turned back into a human.

A few traces of my previous physical powers—mild regeneration, an increased metabolism, nothing special—remained, but I was fine again with sunlight, crosses, garlic, and holy water.

The story isn't worth telling.

It doesn't have your usual happy ending.

It's a finished case, a closed topic. The few remaining things you could consider issues, like having my blood drunk once a month and doing so causing my eyesight and whatnot to supersede human levels every time, are a personal matter at this point, problems that I simply need to confront for the rest of my life.

And anyway—I got off on the lucky side.

It was only over spring break, after all.

My hell was just two weeks long.

Unlike Senjogahara's.

In her case—the case of the girl who met a crab.

She had to deal, for over two years, with a physical inconvenience.

An inconvenience that infringed on her freedom.

Two years of hell—what did that feel like?

So maybe it's no surprise that Senjogahara uncharacteristically feels a sincere debt of gratitude toward me, more than she really needs to—putting aside the physical inconvenience, the resolution of the one that plagued her mind must have been an irreplaceable and invaluable achievement.

Her mind.

Her psyche.

Yes, in the end, problems of that nature, the kind you can't discuss with anyone because no one will understand, shackles, or wedges into, your psyche more than your body—oftentimes.

Just as sunlight peeking through my curtains in the morning still scares me—even though I'm fine now.

As far as I know, there's one other person whom Oshino has helped in the same way, and that's the president of my and Senjogahara's class, Tsubasa Hanekawa—but it was only a few days for her, even shorter than for me, and moreover she's forgotten it. In that sense, you could say hers is the most fortunate position. True, Hanekawa's case is totally beyond saving unless we take such an angle—

"Around here."

"What?"

"The home I used to live in. It was around here."

"Your home—" I looked in the exact direction Senjogahara pointed, but all that stood there was "…a street."

"A street."

It was a fine example of road. The color of the asphalt was still new—as if it had just been paved. Which meant—

"Is this what you'd call residential redevelopment?" I asked.

"The more accurate term here would be town planning."

"You knew?"

"I didn't."

"Then you ought to act more surprised."

"I'm not a very good actor."

Indeed, she hadn't so much as raised an eyebrow.

But—her eyes were fixed in that direction, on that place. From Senjogahara's demeanor, you could, if you wanted to, interpret her as being struck inside with the helpless feeling of having nowhere to go.

"It really has changed—completely. I can't believe it's only been a year."

"………"

"How boring."

It's a shame when we bothered to come, she mumbled.

She sounded truly bored.

But in any case, this must have meant that one of Senjogahara's main objectives for her day out in this area, right up there next to giving her clothes a test drive, or whatever it was she said, had been met.

I turned around.

Mayoi Hachikuji was hiding behind my leg and examining Senjogahara. The girl was silent, as if her guard was up. Despite her being a child, or perhaps because she was a child, she seemed to be able to intuit just how dangerous Senjogahara was and had been using me as a wall for quite a while in order to avoid her. Of course, it's impossible for one person to use another as a wall, so it was obvious she was there, and it

147

was also clear that she was attempting to avoid Senjogahara, to the extent that the situation began to feel awkward for me, a third party. But Senjogahara, for her part, made zero attempts to engage with a mere kid (speaking only to me with her "Over here" or "We're going down this street"), so they were even, so to speak.

It didn't feel great to be stuck in the middle.

Though judging by her reaction, Senjogahara didn't dislike or have trouble being around children as much as she—simply didn't understand them.

"I didn't expect the house to still be there after we sold it, but…I wasn't expecting it to be a road. I have to say, it's making me feel pretty blue."

"Yeah…I guess it would."

All I could do was sympathize.

It was easy to see where she was coming from.

The path from the park to our current location was a mix of roads both old and new, and the neighborhood looked nothing like the guide, the residential map on that park sign—so the sight somehow felt demoralizing even to me, as unattached to the area as I was.

But what can you do?

Towns change, just like people do.

"Phew." Senjogahara let out a big sigh. "I've wasted your time on something pointless. Ready to go, Araragi?"

"Huh…already? Are you sure?"

"I'm sure."

"I see. Okay, then. Let's go, Hachikuji," I said.

Hachikuji nodded silently.

…Maybe she was under the impression that Senjogahara would figure out where she was if she spoke.

Senjogahara began striding off on her own.

Hachikuji and I followed after her.

"Actually, Hachikuji, could you let go of my leg? It's hard for me to walk. You're grabbing onto me like you're a baby koala or something. What're you gonna do if I fall?"

"……"

"Say something, will you?" I demanded.

"Well," Hachikuji responded, "it's not as if I want to hold on to your dreadful leg, Mister Araragi!"

I peeled her off of me.

Rrrrrrip—though there was no sound.

"I can't believe you! I'm telling the PTA about this!" she complained.

"Oh yeah, the PTA?"

"The PTA is an incredible organization! They'd barely have to lift a finger to put a lone, powerless, underage citizen like you down and out for the count, Mister Araragi!"

"Barely a finger, huh? Sounds scary. By the way, do you know what PTA stands for, Hachikuji?"

"Huh? Well…"

Hachikuji sank back into silence. She must not have known.

Of course, I didn't know either.

I was just glad it didn't turn into a long, drawn-out argument.

"PTA stands for Parent-Teacher Association. It's an English term for a school organization made up of guardians and instructors," Senjogahara answered from the front. "It also stands for percutaneous transluminal angioplasty, a medical term. But I doubt that's what you're talking about, Araragi, so the first explanation should be the right one."

"Huh. I'd vaguely known it was some kind of meeting of parents, but I didn't know the teachers counted too. You're quite literate, Senjogahara, aren't you?"

"No, Araragi, it's just that you're an illiterate bum."

"I'll accept the 'illiterate' as an antonym, but the 'bum'…"

"You don't like it? Then let's say 'scum' instead."

She didn't even turn around to face me.

She really seemed to be in a bad mood…

An ordinary person might wonder how Senjogahara was acting any differently from her usual acid-tongued self, but once you've experienced as much verbal abuse from her as I have, you start to get a feel for it. She just wasn't being as sharp. Normally, or even when she's in a good mood, she doesn't let up.

Hmm.

What was it?

Was it because her home had become a road—or was it my fault? It seemed like both.

Whatever it was, though, even putting aside the child abuse aspect, I'd also abandoned Senjogahara mid-conversation to mind Hachikuji… It had felt like the natural thing to do, but Senjogahara couldn't have been happy about it.

In that case, I needed to get this little girl, Mayoi Hachikuji, straight to her destination and then focus on cheering Senjogahara back up. I'd buy her lunch, then go shopping with her—and if time allowed, I'd take her somewhere fun. All right, I decided, that was the plan. I didn't want to head home anyway because of that business with my little sisters, so I'd spend the day attending to Senjogahara. And just my luck, I was carrying a lot of cash—wait, what was I, her slave?!

I managed to surprise even myself.

"By the way, Hachikuji."

"What is it, Mister Araragi?"

"This address," I began, taking her note out of my pocket. I had yet to return it to her. "What exactly is this place?"

And.

What was she going to do there?

I wanted to know so long as I was taking here there—especially considering she was an elementary school girl traveling alone.

"Hah, I'm not telling! I exercise my right to remain silent!"

"………"

What a little smart aleck.

Who ever said kids were pure and innocent?

"No talk, no help," I said.

"I never asked for your help! I can get there myself!"

"Aren't you lost?"

"And what if I am?!"

"Um… So for future reference, Hachikuji, you should ask people for help when you get lost."

"People like you who can't put any faith in themselves, Mister

Araragi, are free to do that! Ask others for help to your heart's content! But I don't have any need for that! This kind of thing is a daily insurance for me!"

"Oh…so I guess your policy covers it."

An odd rejoinder.

But I could see why Hachikuji considered me a nuisance. When I was in elementary school, I believed I could do anything on my own, too. I was convinced there was no need to ever ask for anyone's help—that there was nothing I needed outside assistance to do.

I could do anything?

Yeah.

Of course I couldn't.

"Very well then, young lady. Please, would you be so kind as to bestow upon me the secret of what exactly lies in this location?"

"You don't sound very sincere!"

She was a hard nut to crack.

That move would have been enough for either of my middle school sisters…but Hachikuji's face did have an intelligent cast, and maybe I couldn't treat her like some dumb kid. What to do?

"…All right."

A brilliant idea came to me.

I reached into my back pocket and took out my wallet.

I was carrying a lot of cash.

"I'll give you an allowance, young lady."

"Woo-hoo! I'll tell you anything you want!"

Dumb kid.

Actually, she was really dumb…

I was sure that not a single real child had ever been abducted this way—but Hachikuji seemed to have what it took to be a historic first.

"Someone named Miss Tsunade lives there."

"Tsunade? Is that her last name or something?"

"It's a wonderful last name!" Hachikuji said, sounding upset for some reason.

I could understand feeling annoyed by someone dissing an acquaintance's name, but I didn't see myself ever raising my voice over it. Was she emotionally unstable or something?

"Okay... So how do you know this person?"

"She's a relative."

"A relative, huh?"

In other words, Hachikuji was on her way to go spend her Sunday playing at a close relative's home. Either she had some very hands-off parents, or she had snuck her way here when they weren't looking. I didn't know which—but regardless of her intentions, the solo elementary school weekend adventure had come to a screeching halt.

"Is this a cousin you're friends with? You must've come a long way, judging by how big that backpack is. This is the kind of thing you should do over a longer vacation, like Golden Week. Or is there some specific reason you had to do this today?"

"Yes, something like that."

"It's Mother's Day, you ought to be at home like a good daughter."

Well.

I wasn't in any position to be saying that, of course.

—You know, Koyomi, that's why.

That's why? What was the big issue?

"I don't want to hear that from you, Mister Araragi."

"Hey, what do you know about my situation?!"

"It's just a feeling I have."

"......"

It seemed she didn't have any reasoning to back herself up, but was simply annoyed on an instinctual level that I was lecturing her.

How cruel.

"So what were you doing in a place like that, Mister Araragi? Sitting vacantly on a park bench on a Sunday morning doesn't seem to me like something a respectable human being would do."

"Nothing really. Just—"

Passing the time, I nearly said, before stopping myself at the last second. I'd remembered, any man who answers "just passing the time" when he's asked what he's doing is as good as useless. That was a close call.

"Just doing some bike touring."

"Bike touring? How cool!"

She praised me.

I'd expected that to be followed by something mean, but it never came.

Oh, I thought. So Hachikuji is capable of praising me...

"On a bicycle, not a motorcycle, though."

"Is that so. When I hear 'bike touring,' I assume motorcycles are being discussed! That's very unfortunate! Do you not have a license, Mister Araragi?!"

"Sadly, my school's rules won't let me get a license. But I'd rather wait to drive a car either way, motorcycles are dangerous."

"Is that so. But in that case, wouldn't you be fouring?!"

"........"

Yikes. She was misspelling "touring" in a pretty amusing way. Would it be kinder to correct her or to leave her be? ...I wasn't sure.

Incidentally, Senjogahara showed no reaction as she continued to walk ahead.

She didn't even attempt to participate in the conversation.

Maybe she couldn't hear low-IQ conversations.

Still.

The carefree smile I'd just seen from Mayoi Hachikuji was a rather charming thing. It was a wholehearted smile. To say it was like a flower in bloom might be a cliché, but it was the kind of expression that most people lose the ability to make once they grow up.

"Phew... Jeez."

I'd put myself in a dangerous position once again. Were I a pedophile, my heart would've been won over. Ah, how fortunate that I wasn't one...

"In any case," I said, "the streets around here are really complicated. How do they even work? I can't believe you tried to come here on your own."

"Well, it isn't my first time."

"Oh? Then why did you get lost?"

"...It's been a while," Hachikuji replied in an embarrassed voice.

Hmph...I could see that happening. She thought she could do it,

153

but she couldn't when she tried. You can think something, but that doesn't mean it's true. And that went for elementary schoolers, high schoolers, and anyone else for that matter.

"Speaking of which, Mister Arararagi—"

"That's one too many *ra*'s!"

"I'm sorry. A slip of the tongue."

"Well, don't do it again…"

"I'm not sure what you expect. Everyone misspeaks from time to time. Or do you mean to say that you've never had a slip of the tongue in your entire life, Mister Araragi?"

"I wouldn't say never, but I don't slip up when I'm saying someone's name."

"Okay, then. Say 'She sells sea-shells on the sea-shore' three times in a row."

"That isn't a name."

"Yes, it is. I have three friends named that, in fact. So I would say it's a fairly common name."

She sounded so confident.

It's so easy to see through kids' lies.

Shockingly easy.

"She sells sea-shells on the sea-shore, she sells sea-shells on the sea-shore, she sells sea-shells on the sea-shore."

I did it.

"What are you when your dreams don't come true?" Hachikuji said, not missing a beat.

I was apparently being riddled now. "…Sore?"

"Bzzzt. Wrong!" Hachikuji said with a knowing look. "The answer is…" She wore an intrepid grin. "…Human."

"You think you're so clever!"

I'd screamed in an unnecessarily loud voice because, despite myself, I did find it clever.

But anyway.

We were in what you'd call a sleepy residential area.

We walked but came across no one else. It seemed like the kind of place where anyone with somewhere to go left in the morning—while

154

everyone else stayed inside all day. Of course, that wasn't so different from the area where I lived, but what was different was all the incredibly large homes around us. Everyone who lived in the neighborhood must be rich. And now that I thought about it, I'd been told Senjogahara's father was some big shot at a foreign-owned company. That was probably normal for the people who lived there.

A foreign-owned company, huh?

Not exactly what you'd associate with a town in the middle of nowhere like ours.

"Hey, Araragi," Senjogahara said, speaking for the first time in a while. "Could you give me that address again?"

"Huh? Sure. Is it around here?"

"You might say so, or not," Senjogahara answered vaguely.

Unsure of what that meant, I read the note aloud once more.

Senjogahara nodded in understanding.

"It seems like we've gone too far."

"What? Really?"

"That's what it looks like," Senjogahara said in a calm voice. "If you'd like to criticize me, then go ahead, criticize me to your heart's content."

"…Uh, I wouldn't over something this minor."

What a weird way to act defiant…

She was being gracious and not really accepting.

"Okay."

Senjogahara turned back the way we came, her face showing no signs of agitation whatsoever—and Hachikuji moved in perfect contrast to her, avoiding Senjogahara by rotating around me.

"…Why are you that freaked out by Senjogahara? It's not like she's done anything to you. In fact, I know it might not look like it at first glance, but it's her showing you the way, not me."

I was just tagging along.

I wasn't in a position to act all high and mighty.

Even if Hachikuji's childlike intuition was making her eschew Senjogahara, this was going too far. You could say a lot of things about Senjogahara, but she wasn't made of steel. How could she not be hurt by someone avoiding her so blatantly? Aside from whatever concern I had for Senjogahara, Hachikuji wasn't treating her right on a moral level.

"There's nothing I could say to that..." Hachikuji admitted, surprising me with her modest, timid response.

She continued in a whisper, "Don't you feel it, though, Mister Araragi?"

"Feel what?"

"The brutal malice emanating from that woman..."

"........."

She seemed to be going on something more than intuition.

The worst part was that I couldn't disagree with her.

"She doesn't seem to like me... I can feel a strong will coming from her, and it's saying, 'You're in the way, get lost'..."

"I don't know if I'd go that far, but... Hmm."

Fine.

I'd ask, even though I was a bit scared to.

While the answer seemed obvious to me, it seemed like I needed to get her on the record.

"Hey, Senjogahara."

"What is it?"

Once again, she replied without turning around.

Maybe "You're in the way, get lost" was what she was thinking about me.

It was strange. We considered each other friends, but we had such a hard time getting along.

"Do you not like kids?"

"No, I don't. I hate them. I wish they'd die, every last one of them." Ruthless.

Hachikuji shrank back with an "Eep!"

"I don't have any idea how I'm supposed to deal with them. I think it happened in middle school. I was shopping in a department store when I bumped into a child about seven years old."

"Oh, and you made the kid cry?"

"No, that wasn't the problem. I found myself telling him, 'My goodness, sir, are you all right? Are you injured? I'm sincerely sorry.

Please forgive me.'"

" ...."

"I was thrown off-balance because I didn't know how to talk to little kids. Still, having acted so politely and modestly to one was such a shock to me...that I've decided to show nothing but hatred to anything you'd call a child, human or otherwise."

She was practically taking it out on them.

I understood the logic, but not the sensibility.

"By the way, Araragi."

"What's up?"

"It seems we've gone too far in the wrong direction again."

"Hunh?"

We'd gone too far—past the address?

Really? That made two times in a row.

You could expect someone coming to a new place to have trouble matching locations on a map to where they actually were, but Senjogahara lived here until recently.

"If you'd like to criticize me, then go ahead, try and criticize me to your heart's content."

"No, I wouldn't over something... Hold on a sec. Did you say it slightly differently from the last time?"

"You think? I didn't notice."

"Come on. Oh yeah, weren't you talking about town planning or something earlier? Even your home had become a road, so I guess it'd make sense for this place to look pretty different from how you remember it."

"No. That's not the problem." She looked around the area once more, then continued, "Yes, there are more roads, some houses are gone, and others have been built, but it's not as if all the old streets are gone... There's no structural reason for me to get lost."

"Uh huh..."

Since she really was lost, that did seem to be the case. How could I conclude otherwise? Maybe Senjogahara didn't want to own up to making a careless mistake. She could be pretty obstinate in her own way... But as these thoughts ran through my mind, I heard a "What?" come from her.

"I can tell by your face that you're itching to complain. If there's something you want to say, then why not say it like a man? I'll strip naked and get down on all fours to apologize to you, if that'll make you happy."

"Are you trying to make me out to be the most disgusting man on Earth?"

As if I'd let her do that in the middle of a residential area.

Plus, I wasn't interested in having her grovel in the first place.

"Getting down on all fours naked," she said, "is a small price to pay to make Koyomi Araragi known the world over as the most disgusting man alive."

"Your pride is the only thing here that's cheap."

I could no longer figure out whether she was supposed to be a haughty character or a shameless one.

"But I'd be keeping just my socks on," she added.

"You say that like a punch line to wrap this up, but I'm not into weird stuff."

"And by socks, I mean fishnet tights."

"Getting more extreme doesn't change a thing…"

Though on second thought.

Even if I wasn't into that, a part of me did want to see Senjogahara, specifically, in fishnet tights—she wouldn't even have to be naked. I mean, if she looked like this in regular black stockings…

"That's the face of someone thinking unseemly thoughts, Araragi."

"Who, me? Do you really see me in such a vulgar light, a guy whose motto is 'the straight and narrow'? I can't believe you'd say that about me, Senjogahara."

"Oh? I believe I've always been saying these things about you, whether I have proof or not. It's very suspicious that instead of coming back with some sort of quip, you're rejecting the claim outright."

"Ulp…"

"So forcing me down on all fours to apologize to you naked isn't enough, you want to write obscene things across every inch of my body with permanent marker?"

"I wasn't going that far!"

"Then how far were you going?"

"Um, anyway, Hachikuji," I brusquely changed the topic. I could do worse than borrow a page from Senjogahara's book in that regard. "Sorry, but this might take a little longer. But we know it's in this area, so—"

"No," Hachikuji said in a surprisingly calm tone—the kind of unfeeling, mechanical tone you used in class to supply the answer to an obvious equation. "It's probably impossible."

"What? 'Probably'?"

"If 'probably' isn't pleasing to you, then 'absolutely.'"

"……"

It's not like I wasn't pleased with "probably."

I wasn't pleased with "absolutely," either.

But—I found myself with no reply.

Not to that tone.

"Because no matter how many times we try, I'll never get there."

Hachikuji.

"I'll never get there."

Hachikuji repeated herself.

"I'll never get there—to my mother."

Just like—a broken record.

Like a record, unbroken.

"Because I'm—a lost snail."

005

"A Lost Cow," Mèmè Oshino said in the low growl of a man who had been forced awake from a thousand years of sealed, peaceful slumber, as unbelievably grumpy as he was groggy. He wasn't anemic, as far as I knew, but he still seemed to have an awful time waking up. The difference between the way he was speaking to us at that moment and his usual banter was striking.

"That'd be a Lost Cow there."

"A cow? No, I said a snail."

"You know how 'snail' is written in characters. There's a cow in there, right? Don't tell me you write it phonetically. You have such a low IQ, Araragi. Take the character for 'whirlpool' and substitute the left-hand 'water' with 'insect.' Then add 'cow' as a second character."

"Oh, I think I get it now."

"That first character is barely ever used in any word other than 'snail.' A snail's shell forms a spiral, doesn't it? That must be it. It's also close to one of the characters used in 'calamity,' though…and maybe that one is the more symbolic? There are a countless number of aberrations out there that cause humans to lose their way. In terms of Japanese *yokai* that block your path, you must have heard of the *nuri-kabe*… If it's one of those and it's a snail, it has to be the Lost Cow. You see, its name describes its nature, not its form. Whether it's a cow or a snail, it's all the same. As for the form, you can even find some paintings of the thing looking like a human… Araragi, the person who comes up with a name for an aberration and the person who comes up with what that aberration looks like are rarely the same. You could even say never—in most cases, the name comes first. More the concept than the name, actually. Think of it as the illustrations in a light novel. The concept exists before it's visualized—they say that names give shape to nature, but 'nature' in this instance doesn't mean physical, outward appearance. It means essence, so…gaah."

He seemed very sleepy.

Then again, that sleepiness had rid him of his normal frivolity to the point that I found it easier to talk to him. Talking to Oshino is, if anything, tiring.

A snail.

A shelled pulmonate, classified under Mollusca Gastropoda.

You see slugs more often than snails, but those are really just shell-less snails.

Pour salt on them—and they melt.

After that.

I, Koyomi Araragi, and Hitagi Senjogahara, along with Mayoi Hachikuji, retried and used a total of five continues. We tried shortcuts that skirted the edges of the law, we tried demoralizingly long detours, we tried everything we could think of, but, to cut to the chase, everything ended up being a spectacular waste of time. We knew we had to be near our destination—but we couldn't reach it, for whatever reason. In the end, we even tried using brute force, checking every home one by one, but that too got us nowhere.

So as a last resort, Senjogahara booted up a special navigation system feature on her phone (don't ask me about the details) that used GPS or whatever—

But she lost signal moments before the data loaded.

At that point, I finally—or maybe unwillingly—had a perfect grasp on what was up. Senjogahara seemed to have noticed fairly early on, without saying so—and Hachikuji most likely understood the situation better than either of us, but putting that aside.

A demon for me.

A cat for Hanekawa.

A crab for Senjogahara.

It seemed for Hachikuji, it was a snail.

That meant—I was no longer in a position to give up on the matter. With an ordinary lost child, if I couldn't help her myself, I'd hand her over to a neighborhood police station and smugly consider the case closed. But if it involved *that world*—

Senjogahara was also against handing Hachikuji off to the police.

Senjogahara—who had been steeped in that world for a few years.

If Senjogahara said so—there was no mistaking it.

Of course, it wasn't a problem that Senjogahara and I could attend to on our own—it wasn't as if either of us had any apropos special abilities. It was just a case of us *knowing* that there was another side, one that wasn't ours.

You can say knowledge is power.

But you're powerless if knowledge is all you have.

Which is why—Senjogahara and I went with the safe, easy choice, not our first, but after some discussion, our final choice, of asking Oshino what to do.

Mèmè Oshino.

My—our savior.

If not for that, he's certainly the kind of man I wouldn't want to associate with. Past thirty but still lacking a fixed address, he was sleeping for over a month now in a bankrupt cram school. That description alone would be enough to drive away any normal person.

—I'm interested in this town for the time being.

That was his excuse.

So there's no telling when he might disappear. He's a rolling stone, the real deal, but Senjogahara and I had gone to him just last Monday about her problem—as well as on Tuesday, to deal with loose ends. I, myself, had seen him the day before, too. Considering all that, I was sure he would still be in that abandoned building.

That meant the only problem was getting in touch with him.

He doesn't own a cell phone.

Our only choice was to go and see him in person.

I wouldn't say Senjogahara has much of a relationship with him, since they only met the week before. Being more familiar with Oshino, it felt like I should be the one to go see him, but Senjogahara spoke up, saying, "I'll go."

"Let me borrow your mountain bike," she said.

"If you want, sure...but do you know how to get there? I can draw you a map if you want—"

"It doesn't make me glad in the slightest to have someone with a memory as poor as yours worrying over me. If anything, it's making me feel sad."

"...Is that so."

I started to feel sad.

Really, actually, sad.

"To be honest," she told me, "I wanted to try riding this mountain bike from the moment I saw it in the parking lot."

"So you weren't kidding when you were talking about how incredible mountain bikes are... I was convinced you didn't mean it. You're not very good at sounding honest, you know."

"Or rather," Senjogahara said, then practically whispered in my ear, "don't leave me alone with her."

"........."

"I wouldn't know what to do with her."

Yeah, that did seem true.

True for Hachikuji, too.

I handed the key to my mountain bike over to Senjogahara. I remembered hearing that she didn't own a bike, so it did seem dangerous to be lending my oh-so-beloved ride—but since it was Senjogahara, I figured why not.

So.

I now found myself waiting for Senjogahara to contact us.

I was back in the park with the ambiguous pronunciation and sitting on a bench.

Next to me was Mayoi Hachikuji.

Where she sat, another person could have fit in between us.

It was as if she wanted to be able to make a break for it.

In fact, she seemed ready to.

I'd already told Hachikuji a bit about my own and Senjogahara's past, and continuing, circumstances—but this only seemed to heighten her guard. I'd made a poor decision that backfired on me after everything I'd done to get her to open up—and now all I could do was start over from the beginning.

Trust is a very important thing, after all.

Sigh…

I'd try talking to her.

There was something I was wondering about, anyway.

"Hey, a little earlier—I want to say you were talking about your mother? What did you mean by that? Wasn't this Miss Tsunade a relative of yours?"

"…"

She didn't reply.

She was exercising her right to remain silent.

What I'd tried before might not work this time… It only did as a joke anyway, and if I repeated it too often, people might think I meant it—and by people, I mean myself.

And so.

"Hey, Hachikuji. I'll get you some ice cream, so will you come a little closer?"

"I'm coming!"

Hachikuji sidled up to me right away.

…It seemed like she didn't mind taking me at my word and waiting until later for her payment.

Speaking of which, I hadn't given her a single yen of allowance yet, either… What an easy girl to control.

"So, what I was talking about," I resumed.

"What was that again?"

"About—your mother."

"……"

She exercised her right to remain silent.

I continued on, unfazed. "Were you lying when you said you were going to a relative's?"

165

"…I wasn't lying," Hachikuji said, pouting. "Your mother counts as a relative, doesn't she?"

"Sure, technically, but…"

It felt like splitting hairs.

And in any case—a girl carrying a backpack to head to her mother's home alone on a Sunday was something of an odd situation…

"Also," she continued, still pouting, "while I call her my mother, sadly she isn't my mother anymore."

"…Oh."

A divorce.

She lived with her father.

It was a story I'd heard—just the other day.

I'd heard it from Senjogahara.

"My last name was Tsunade until I was in third grade. But it changed to Hachikuji when my father started looking after me."

"Huh? Hold on."

It was getting complicated, and I decided to take a moment to sort it out. Hachikuji was currently in fifth grade, and her last name until third grade was Tsunade (which must be why she cared enough about the name to yell at me), but it changed to Hachikuji once her father took her in. That meant… A-ha, so when her parents married, they decided to take her mother's last name. In Japan a couple had to have the same surname once they got married, but it could be the man's or the woman's. Which meant…when her parents got divorced, her mother—Miss Tsunade—left their home and moved to this neighborhood… or more likely moved back in with her own parents. And that's why—Hachikuji was here on a Sunday.

She was taking advantage of Mother's Day.

To visit her mother—was that it?

Her name was—a precious gift from her father and mother.

"Yikes…and I'd tried to lecture you as your senior about being a better daughter…"

No wonder she didn't want to be told.

Talk about being an annoyance.

"No, it doesn't have anything to do with today being Mother's Day.

Her home is a place I'd visit anytime, if I had the opportunity."

"...I see."

"But I never get there."

"........."

After the divorce, her mother left home.

She couldn't meet her mother.

But Hachikuji wanted to.

So she came to see her.

Attempted to.

Carrying her backpack—and then.

And then—a snail came along.

"And that was when you encountered it," I said.

"I don't know what I did."

"Huh."

Ever since then—no matter how many times she tried to visit her mother.

Hachikuji couldn't get there, not once.

I knew it'd be insensitive to ask how many times she'd tried and if she'd really failed every time—and the fact that she hadn't given up was impressive.

It was impressive—but.

"......"

It's not the best way to put it—nor should I be comparing it to other people's experiences, I thought, but this feels much less dangerous than the problems that Hanekawa, Senjogahara, and I went through. It was neither a physical nor a psychological issue, but a phenomenological one where she couldn't do something that she should be able to. The problem didn't reside in her.

It was external.

It didn't endanger her existence.

Her day-to-day life wasn't severely impacted.

Which is why I felt the way I did.

But then again, even if that was true, I shouldn't lord it over Hachikuji—no matter what. I had no right to say anything of the sort to her, regardless of what I'd gone through over spring break.

So all I told her was, "You know—sounds like you've been through a lot, too."

The words came from the bottom of my heart.

I nearly wanted to pat her on the head.

So I did.

"Grrah!"

She bit my hand.

"Ow! What the hell are you doing, you little brat?!"

"Grrrrrrrgh!"

"Ow! Ow, ow, oww!"

Sh-She wasn't joking, she wasn't playing around, she wasn't covering up her embarrassment, she was honestly biting down on my hand as hard as she could… I didn't have to look at my hand to know that her teeth had pierced my skin and entered into my flesh, or that I was gushing blood! This was no laughing matter. Why had she suddenly—or had I unwittingly triggered some sort of event without knowing it?

Did that mean a battle had begun?!

I balled my unbitten hand into a fist. As if I was crushing the air out of it. Then, I took that fist and drove it directly into the pit of Hachikuji's stomach. The solar plexus is a major weak spot on any human body. Amazingly, Hachikuji kept her teeth firmly inside my hand, but she couldn't help easing up for a moment. I used this opening to swing the arm that hand was connected to in every direction with all my might. Hachikuji had all but bitten off a chunk of my hand, but this had left the rest of her body open—and sure enough, it was hoisted off the bench.

I opened my fist and attempted to hold her defenseless torso in my hand—for a fifth grader, she felt surprisingly plump in my palm, but this fact had little to no influence on me as I was not a pedophile, which meant that I was able to use that momentum to flip her over. She was still biting my hand, causing her body to get wrenched at her neck. But that wasn't a problem; so long as her teeth were inside my hand, there was a risk that any attacks to her head would deal damage to me as well. What was important was that this exposed Hachikuji's torso as if she were a set of carefully stacked tiles at a karate demonstration. I aimed, of course, at the target of my previous strike, her solar plexus!

"Ghhak—"

It was over.

Hachikuji finally dislodged her teeth from my hand.

As she did, something resembling stomach acid came pouring out of her mouth.

And then—she passed right out.

"Heh—wait, that wasn't funny."

I shook my bitten hand as if to loosen it up.

"What an empty thing victories are after the first…"

There he sat, a high school boy acting like a dispassionate nihilist, having just knocked out an elementary school girl by punching her twice in a human's vital spot, along the median line.

Hold on, that was me too.

……

Sure, I could understand smacking her, grabbing her, and tossing her, but hitting a girl with a balled fist? Seriously?

There was no need for Koyomi Araragi to have Hitagi Senjogahara apologize to him on all fours while naked. He already had what it took to be an awful human being.

"Agh… Still, I didn't know she was one to chomp on people out of nowhere."

I decided to take a look at the bite wound.

Wow, yikes… I could see my bones… I never knew that could happen when a human being bit another hard enough.

Of course, this was me we were talking about.

The wound might have hurt, but it wasn't so serious that it wouldn't heal immediately—*without any special care at all.*

It crawled and oozed shut—at a speed visible to the eye, almost as if it were taking place in fast forward, or rewind, and when I saw that—it made me realize all over again how much of a wrong turn my life had taken. I began to feel down—even gloomy, all over again.

Honestly—how small I was.

An awful person, in my state? I made myself laugh.

I actually thought I'd turned back into a human?

"...Ooh, what a scary look that is on your face, Araragi," a voice abruptly called out to me.

I thought it was Senjogahara for a moment—but it couldn't be. Her words would never sound so sunny.

There stood the class president.

Tsubasa Hanekawa.

The fact that she was wearing the exact uniform she wore to school despite it being a Sunday must have been natural for her, part of her charm as a model student—her hair and her glasses were the same as well, and the only difference in her appearance I could detect compared to when she was at school was a handbag she carried.

"H-Hanekawa."

"You look surprised. Well, I guess that's preferable."

Heh heh heh—Hanekawa showed a smile.

Yes, just like the one I'd seen on Hachikuji's face a moment earlier—

"What's going on?" Hanekawa asked. "Why are you here, of all places?"

"W-Well—I should be asking you the same question."

There was no way I could hide how shaken I was.

The only question remaining was how long she'd been watching.

If Tsubasa Hanekawa, the embodiment of decency, the breathing textbook of moral behavior, the living exemplar of purity, had witnessed me inflicting violence upon a grade school girl, that spelled trouble, but in a completely different way than if Senjogahara had seen me do the same...

I didn't want to get expelled during my last year of high school...

"What do you mean, asking me? I'm from this area. If anyone deserves the question, it's you, Araragi. Do you sometimes come over here?"

"Um."

Oh, right.

Senjogahara and Hanekawa had gone to the same middle school.

And it was a public school, which meant—of course. Considering how school districts were drawn, it wasn't odd at all for Senjogahara's old home turf and Hanekawa's habitat to overlap. Though they must not have matched perfectly, because it sounded like they'd gone to separate elementary schools…

"Not really, but, well, I didn't have anything to do, so I was just passing the time here—"

Oops.

I'd said I was "just passing the time."

"Ha hah. Just passing the time? Sounds nice. It's nice to not have anything to do. It means you're free. I guess you could say I'm just passing the time, too."

"……"

She and Senjogahara were fundamentally dissimilar organisms.

Or maybe it was the difference between someone who was smart and someone who was the smartest?

"You know, Araragi. It's hard for me to be at home. And the library isn't open on Sundays, so I walk around all day instead. It's good for my health, too."

"…You don't have to try so hard to be considerate."

Tsubasa Hanekawa.

The girl with a pair of mismatched wings.

At school she's an embodiment of decency, a breathing textbook of moral behavior, a living exemplar of purity, a class president among class presidents, a flawless girl—but her home is a troubled one.

Troubled, as well as warped.

Which is why—she was bewitched by a cat.

It found its way through the smallest crack in her heart.

Perhaps it was an instance of the fact that nobody is totally perfect, but—while the problem was solved and she was freed from the cat, while her memories had vanished, the troubledness and warpedness of her home had not.

It was still troubled, still warped.

"It's kind of embarrassing to have your local library closed on Sundays, though, isn't it? It's like a symbol of how uncultured your area is."

"I don't even know where my local library is."

"That's no good, you shouldn't sound so resigned. You still have time to study for entrance exams, Araragi. You can do it if you try."

"You know, Hanekawa, groundless encouragement can sometimes hurt worse than having insults yelled at you."

"But aren't you good at math, Araragi? Normally, people who can do math do well in other subjects, too."

"You don't have to memorize all that much for math. It's easier on me."

"Boy, are you difficult. Oh, whatever. We'll just take this step by step. By the way, Araragi. Is that girl your little sister?"

Hanekawa's lips grew pointy, and with them she indicated Hachikuji, who was laid out near the bench.

"…My little sisters aren't this tiny."

"They aren't?"

"They're in middle school."

"Huh."

"Um, she's lost. Her name's Mayoi Hachikuji."

"Mayoi?"

"Like the character for 'truth' and the character for 'dusk.' As far as her last name—"

"I know her last name. 'Hachikuji' is a pretty common term in the Kansai region, anyway. Yeah, I think there's a temple in *Shinonome Monogatari* that—oh, actually, it might have been written in a different way there."

"…You know everything, don't you?"

"Not everything. I just know what I know."

"Is that so."

"Hm. 'Mayoi' and 'Hachikuji'—what a poetic name. Hnn? Oh, she's up."

This made me look at Hachikuji, who was slowly blinking her eyes. She seemed to take a muddled yet meticulous look at her surroundings before finally sitting up.

"Hello there, Mayoi. My name's Tsubasa Hanekawa, and I'm friends with this nice guy over here!"

Wow. The public TV children's show voice came natural to her.

Hanekawa must be the kind of person who uses baby talk with dogs and cats and thinks nothing of it…

Hachikuji replied, "Please don't speak to me. I don't like you."

...So she used that line on everyone.

"Hmm? Did I do something to make you hate me? You shouldn't say such things to people you're meeting for the first time, Mayoi. There, there."

Hanekawa seemed completely unfazed.

Unlike me, she was even patting Hachikuji's head like it was no big deal.

"So you like kids, Hanekawa?"

"Hmm? Is there anyone who doesn't?"

"Hey, I'm not saying I don't."

"Ah. Yes, I do like them. It makes me feel all warm and fuzzy to think that this is how I used to be."

There there—Hanekawa continued to pat Hachikuji's head.

Hachikuji tried to resist.

But resistance was futile.

"Ur, urrr..."

"You're such a cutie, Mayoi! I could just eat you right up. Look at your fluffy little cheeks. Ooh! But you know..."

Hanekawa's tone shifted.

To one that she occasionally used with me at school.

"You shouldn't bite his hand for no reason at all. He's going to be just fine, but if he were a normal person, that would have really hurt! Bad girl!"

Whack.

She hit her. With her fist. And not as a joke.

"Urr...ur, urr?"

Having been coddled, then smacked, Hachikuji seemed to be in a state of delirium, and Hanekawa turned her around to make her face me.

"Now say you're sorry."

"...I-I'm sorry for what I did, Mister Araragi."

She apologized.

Hachikuji, who spoke politely but was an obnoxious brat.

It shocked me.

Still, Hanekawa had been watching me for a while… Right, of course, if you thought about it, you had a right to defend yourself when someone bit you hard enough to gouge your flesh. In fact, our first fight, too, had started with her kicking me…

Hanekawa wasn't one to bend the rules, but she wasn't such a stickler for them, either.

She was just fair.

I had to hand it to Hanekawa, though. She knew how to deal with kids. Her performance was impressive, especially because I was sure she didn't have any siblings.

Watching this also made me realize that Hanekawa treated me like a kid when we were at school, but we could put that fact aside for now.

"And you too, Araragi! You've been a bad boy."

She was using the same tone on me.

Maybe we couldn't put the fact aside.

Having noticed what she'd done, Hanekawa cleared her throat and tried again.

"Anyway, don't do that."

"Don't do… Don't be violent, I suppose?"

"No. You need to scold her properly."

"Hm? Oh."

"Violence is bad too, of course. But if you hit a child, or if you hit anyone for that matter, you need to give them a sensible reason."

"……"

"What I'm trying to say is talk, because they'll understand."

"…You know, I learn a lot talking to you."

Wow.

She's such an antidote.

Good people exist in the world.

It lifts me up just to think that.

"So she's lost? Where's she trying to go? Somewhere around here? In that case, I should be able to show her the way."

"Er—no, it's fine. Senjogahara just went to ask someone for help."

While Hanekawa had coped with the other side too, she had no memories of it—if she did, they were also forgotten. There was no need for me to poke at them like I was picking at a scab.

Though her offer was much appreciated, and all.

"She's been taking her sweet time, but she should be back soon," I said.

"What? Senjogahara? You were with Senjogahara, Araragi? Hmm? Senjogahara hasn't been coming to school lately, but—hmm? Oh, now that you mention it, you were asking me all about Senjogahara the other day, weren't you—hmm."

Uh oh.

She was getting suspicious. Real suspicious.

Hanekawa's single-minded-delusion power was bursting at the seams.

"Oh! I see what's going on!" she exclaimed.

"No, I don't think you do…"

A fool like me shooting down an answer that a brilliant person like her came up with felt so wrong, but…

"You know, your fantasizing skills outclass even *yaoi* fangirls."

"*Yaoi*? What's that?" Hanekawa asked, head tilted.

The model student didn't know our native term for slash fiction.

"It's short for 'no climax, no denouement, profound meaning,'" I told her wrong on purpose.

"I think you're lying. Fine. I'll look it up later."

"As serious as ever, I see."

………

I began to worry. What if I had just sent Hanekawa down a dark path?

Would it be my fault?

"Well, I don't want to be a nuisance, so I'll be on my way," she announced. "Sorry for the bother, and say hello to Senjogahara for me. Though I won't get on your case too much about it because it's a Sunday, don't slack off too much. Plus, don't forget that there's a history quiz tomorrow. Plus, we're going to have to start getting serious about preparing for the culture festival, so get yourself ready, okay? Plus—"

Hanekawa continued with nine more of those.

She was like the most positive person ever.

"Oh, that's right, Hanekawa. Just in case, do you mind if I ask you something before you go? Do you know of a Miss Tsunade's home around here?"

"Miss Tsunade? Hmm, well—"

Hanekawa made a show of trying to remember. She did such a good job I started to get my hopes up that she really knew, but then—

"...No, I don't," she said.

"So there are some things you don't know."

"Like I told you. I just know what I know. Outside of that, I'm clueless."

"Is that so."

True, she didn't know what *yaoi* was either.

It wasn't going to be that easy.

"I'm sorry I couldn't live up to your expectations."

"No, no."

"All right. Bye-bye, and I mean it this time," Tsubasa Hanekawa said and left the park.

I wondered. Did she know how to read the park's name?

If there was anything I should've asked her, a part of me thought, that was it.

And then—I received a call on my phone.

An eleven-digit number appeared on its liquid-crystal screen.

"........."

Sunday, May fourteenth, 14:15:30 p.m.

That was the moment I acquired Senjogahara's cell phone number.

006

"So—what kind of spirit, specter, ghoul, or goblin is this Lost Cow, anyway? What do we need to do to defeat it?"

"Really, Araragi, all you ever think about is violence. Something good happen to you lately?"

It seemed as though Senjogahara had woken Oshino up while he was sleeping. He grumbled something about how awful she was to interrupt his lazy Sunday morning, but even putting aside the fact that it was already the afternoon, every day for Oshino was a summer break Sunday. He had no constitutionally guaranteed right to speak those words, so I didn't bother dignifying them with a response.

Oshino had no cell phone, which meant he had to borrow Senjogahara's for us to communicate. However, due to reasons both dogmatic and monetary, he also seemed to be quite bad with technology. When I heard him start saying things as idiotic as, "Hey, tsundere girl. Which button do I press when I'm talking?" I felt an urge to press the button that'd cut the call.

What did he think he was using, a walkie-talkie?

"But...I do wonder what's going on here. This isn't so much uncommon as abnormal. I can't believe you've managed to run into this many aberrations in such a short period of time, Araragi. How funny. Getting attacked by a vampire would be enough for most people, but look at you. First you get yourself mixed up with missy class president's cat, then missy tsundere's crab, and now you've gone and stumbled upon a snail?"

"I'm not the one who did the stumbling."

"Hm? Really?"

"How much did Senjogahara tell you?"

"Well…she did tell me everything, but I was also half-asleep. It's all a bit vague, and I might be misremembering some of it… Oh, but you know, I've always dreamed about how great it would be if a cute high school girl came and woke me up. Thanks to you, Araragi, a dream I've had since middle school has come true at last."

"…And how does it feel?"

"Hmm, I'm not sure. I'm still only half-awake."

Maybe that's how fulfilled dreams are.

Not just for him, but for everyone.

"Hey, she's glaring at me, hard. Yeesh, now I'm scared. I wonder if something good happened to her."

"Who knows."

"Not you, huh? After all, you don't seem like you understand women very well, Araragi—but forget about that. Hm. Well, it is true that it's easier to find yourself back in the world after you've gotten involved in it once, but…it does feel a bit too concentrated. Missy class president and missy tsundere are both your classmates, too—and, from what I understand, they're both from the area you're in, right?"

"Senjogahara doesn't live here anymore, though. But that doesn't have anything to do with this. Hachikuji wouldn't have ever lived here before."

"Hachikuji?"

"Oh, did she not tell you? The name of the girl who came across the snail. Mayoi Hachikuji."

"Ah…"

There was a pause.

It didn't seem to be because he was sleepy, either.

"Mayoi Hachikuji, you say… Ha hah, of course. I'm starting to get the picture. My memories are coming together. Of course. It's a nice little connection, actually. Almost like a play on words."

"A play on words? Oh, because 'mayoi' can mean 'lost'? 'Lost' as in 'Lost Cow' and 'lost child'... You know, Oshino, you come up with some pretty boring ideas for someone who always has such a dumb smile on his face."

"You wouldn't catch me dead making jokes that simple. I don't smile like I do just for show. Nothing conceals a weapon better than a smiling face, you know. I'm talking about both of her names together. Mayoi and Hachikuji. You know, Hachikuji. Like in the fifth verse of *Shinonome Monogatari*?"

"What?"

Hadn't Hanekawa said something similar?

Not that it meant anything to me.

"You don't know anything, Araragi, do you? I'm glad you're giving me a good excuse to explain it all. But we don't have time for that right now, do we? Besides, I'm sleepy. Hm? What's that, missy tsundere?"

Our conversation stopped for a moment as Senjogahara seemed to say something to Oshino. Even my hearing couldn't pick it up— or rather, she was intentionally speaking to him so that I couldn't hear her.

Was she sharing a secret? No—that couldn't be it.

What could she be saying?

"Hmm... Okay."

Oshino nodding along was all I could catch. And—

"...Ahh."

A heavy sigh.

"You really are useless, Araragi. You know that?"

"Huh? What did I do to deserve that from you? I haven't even told you that I'm just passing the time."

"You've made missy tsundere fuss over you so much...she even feels responsible for you. How pathetic. She practically has to hold your hand and dress you, Araragi. It's her who should be wearing the pants here."

"Hold on... I do feel bad about dragging Senjogahara into this. I really do. Not just bad, I feel responsible. It was only last week she finished up taking care of her own problems, but I've already gotten her into another strange—"

"Ugh, that's not what I mean. You know, Araragi, I'm starting to think you're getting a big head after having solved problems with three aberrations in a row. Just to make sure you know, what you, yourself, see and feel isn't the whole truth."

"…I wasn't trying to dispute that."

They were stern words—withering. It felt like he'd hit me where it hurt most, because that did ring a bell.

"Well, you probably don't mean to be doing it, Araragi. I already understand what kind of person you are. I just think it wouldn't hurt if you were a little more considerate, that's all. If you're not acting conceited, then I think something might have you boxed in. Listen carefully. Seeing shouldn't necessarily be believing—and on the flip side, not seeing isn't necessarily counterfactual, Araragi. I want to say I told you something similar the first time we met. I hope you haven't forgotten already."

"…We're not talking about me right now, Oshino. Can you just tell me how to deal with this…Lost Cow? This snail? What do we do to defeat it?"

"Again with the violent talk. Don't say that kind of stuff. You really don't understand a thing, do you? You'll come to regret it if you keep going on like that, and I hope you'll be taking responsibility then. Got that? And also—the Lost Cow is…oh, er."

Oshino hesitated for a moment.

"Ha hah. I don't know, this is just *too simple*. It feels like no matter what I say, I'm going to be saving you here. That's no good… I need you to get saved on your own."

"It's simple? Really?"

"We're not dealing with a vampire here. That really, truly was a rare case, Araragi. I guess you can't help but get a lot of wrong ideas if that was your first experience, but…okay, we could say that this Lost Cow is more like the crab that missy tsundere encountered."

"Hm."

The crab.

That crab.

"Oh, right. About her, too…" Oshino said. "I don't know if I like this. I'm only here to connect humans with the other side. Connecting humans with other humans isn't my specialty, you see… Ha hah. Well then. Now what? I may have let myself get a little too friendly with you, Araragi. It's like we're colluding. I never imagined that it'd be this simple for you to ask me for help, let alone that you'd get me to solve a case for you over the phone."

"…Well, I do think it was too facile of me."

It was easier—and I'd been reluctant about the option.

Still—it was also true that it was the only option.

"I wish you wouldn't treat me in such a casual way. You normally wouldn't have someone like me around when you encounter an aberration. And, though this is such a plain and commonsense thing to say that it's out of character for me to be saying it, I don't think it's very admirable of you to be sending a fine young woman into a more-or-less-abandoned building where a suspicious man is camped out."

"Oh, so you do realize that you're suspicious and that you live in a more-or-less-abandoned building…"

But—I had to admit, he was right. Absolutely right. Senjogahara had agreed to go so readily—she pretty much volunteered—that I failed to be considerate in that regard.

"It's not like you're going to do anything to her."

"While I appreciate the trust you put in me, you do have to draw lines. That's why we have rules. Let them slip out of your hands and soon you'll find yourself in a sloppy situation. Got that? You need to establish boundaries that say no matter the circumstances, this is off limits. Because if you don't, you'll find yourself slowly ceding your ground. You hear people say that rules are made to be broken, but they're not supposed to be. They're rules. Not only that, you won't have anything to break if you don't have rules in the first place. Ha hah, I'm starting to sound like li'l missy class president."

"Mmgh…"

Well—he was right.

Absolutely right.

I'd apologize to Senjogahara later.

"Araragi, it's not as if she trusts me as much as you trust me. All she has is a provisional trust based on the fact that you trust me—so remember, that means if something happens to her, the responsibility falls directly on you. Not that I'd do anything, of course. No, really, I won't! Whoa, please, put down that stapler!"

"……"

So she still carried one of those around.

Then again, that wasn't the kind of habit you got rid of overnight.

"Phew… What a surprise. I guess missy tsundere is a scary missy tsundere, huh? What a case we have here. Well, okay… Eh, you know, I don't like phones after all. It's so hard to talk on them."

"Hard? Seriously? I know some people are bad with technology, but Oshino, that's pushing it."

"Sure, that's a part of it, but it's just that while I'm over here being all serious, you might be lying down, drinking a soda, and reading a manga over there. Everything feels so empty when I think about that."

"Wow…I never knew you were that sensitive."

Apparently, people who minded such things really minded them.

"All right, Araragi, then this is what I'll do. I'll tell her how to deal with the Lost Cow, and you can stay right there."

"How to deal with it? So secondhand knowledge is all we're going to need here?"

"If you're going to put it that way, the Lost Cow itself is oral tradition."

"That's not what I'm trying to get at—um, we don't need some kind of ceremony like we did for Senjogahara?"

"Nope. The pattern here is the same, but this snail isn't as tough to deal with as that crab. It's not a god, after all. It's just a monster, so to speak. And not as in a ghoul or a goblin. It's sort of like a ghost."

"A ghost?"

In this case, I didn't see much of a difference between gods, ghouls, goblins, and ghosts. But this was Oshino I was talking to. I knew that the differences between each were important.

Still—a ghost.

"Ghosts are a kind of yokai, too. The Lost Cow itself isn't unique to any one region, it appears all across Japan. An aberration that's been handed down in every corner of the country. It's not a well-known one, and its name changes here and there, but it started out as a snail. Umm, and one more thing, Araragi. Hachikuji is actually a term that originally referred to temples that stand in bamboo groves. The 'ji' means temple, of course, but the 'hachi-ku' isn't the numbers eight and nine that we tend to write that with. Correctly, it derives from the word for black bamboo. You know that there are two major types in Japan, don't you? Black bamboo and tortoise-shell bamboo. Anyway, this got changed to the characters for 'eight' and 'nine' as, well, just a play on words. Do you know about the eighty-eight-temple pilgrimage in Shikoku, or the thirty-three-temple pilgrimage in the western region?"

"Oh… Well sure, even I've heard of that."

You hear about those all the time.

"Okay, so that's the kind of thing that even you've heard of—sure, I guess it would be. Well, there are a lot of similar pilgrimages, just not all as famous. And one of them is a 'Hachikuji' pilgrimage—with a list of eighty-nine temples. It also has to do with bamboo groves like I said, but in terms of things getting tacked on, they wanted a pilgrimage with one more temple than Shikoku's eighty-eight."

"Huh…"

So it had something to do with Shikoku, the smallest of Japan's four major islands?

But Hanekawa had said something about the western Kansai region of the main island.

"Yep," Oshino said, "because these eighty-nine temples are mostly in Kansai—in that sense, you could say it's closer to the thirty-three-temple pilgrimage than the eighty-eight. But—and here we get to the crux of the story, to where the tragedy begins—you can also easily read the characters for 'eight' and 'nine' together not as 'hachiku' but as 'yaku,' misfortune. Slap that title on your temple and you've added a negative prefix. It wasn't a good idea."

"…? Now that you mention it, I wasn't able to read that part of her name at first and thought it might be 'yaku,' but…it's not as if they meant it that way, right?"

"No, but without meaning to, they gave it that sense. Words are scary things. Without any intention involved at all, things can turn out a certain way. Language is alive, though people say that too casually these days. In any case, the interpretation spread, and it wasn't long until the eighty-nine temples stopped being grouped together. Most of them shut down during the anti-Buddhist movement in the 1800s, anyway, and only about a quarter still exist today—in addition, nearly all of them hide the fact they were ever a part of those eighty-nine temples to begin with."

"......"

His explanations were so offhanded, which made them easy to follow, but I also got the feeling that repeating them to anyone ran the risk of getting mud on my face.

This was the kind of knowledge that didn't turn up a single hit when you searched it online, and I had trouble deciding how much of it I should swallow in the first place.

It called for a grain of salt.

"And so, if you look at the name Mayoi Hachikuji against that background—that history—it seems, well, a little too meaningful for comfort. The names are connected—you see? You find that sort of thing in classical literature, like in *The Great Mirror*, which must have come up in class. Still, I'm not sure about her given name. Mayoi—'lost'? It seems too obvious. If anything here is facile or simplistic, that'd be it. Whoever came up with it doesn't seem to have a knack for names. Hm, it'd have been good if you sensed this from the beginning, Araragi."

"Good? What? And also—"

Hachikuji was sitting on the bench, waiting patiently for me to finish the call. It didn't look like she was listening in on me—but she had to be. The conversation was about her, how could she not?

"It wasn't until recently that her last name became Hachikuji. It was Tsunade before that."

"Tsunade? Huh, really now… Throw that kink into the mix—and the thread starts to get tangled. Frayed, you could say. That's a little too much, even for fate. Like there's a man behind the curtains pulling the strings so that all the dominoes can fall. Hachikuji and Tsunade… I see, and then Mayoi. So that was the important one here. Ma-yoi—'true twilight.' Phew—gimme a break."

How ridiculous, Oshino muttered.

He said it as though to himself—but it was intended for me.

"You know what, Araragi, it doesn't matter. This is a really interesting town, I have to say. A motley crucible. I get the feeling I won't be able to leave for a while... Well, I'll tell missy tsundere the details, so you get them from her."

"Hm? O-Okay."

"That is—" Oshino wrapped up in a tone so sarcastic I could practically see his smirk, "if you're lucky enough for her to come out and tell you."

And then—the call ended.

Oshino had a rule about never saying goodbyes.

"...So, Hachikuji. Looks like there's a way."

"It didn't sound like there is, going by your conversation."

So she'd been listening.

Well, she couldn't have figured out the important parts if she'd only heard my side of it.

"At any rate, Mister Araragi."

"What is it?"

"You do realize that I'm hungry, right?"

".........."

Okay, so what?

Don't say that, I thought, like you're gently trying to let me know I've forgotten to fulfill an important obligation.

But now that she mentioned it, I'd forgotten thanks to this snail business that I hadn't seen to Hachikuji's lunch. Senjogahara, too... In her case, though, she may have gone off to eat somewhere on her own before heading to Oshino's place.

Huh, it hadn't occurred to me.

Because my body no longer required me to eat much.

"Okay, then let's go somewhere to eat once Senjogahara gets back. Actually, there's only homes around here—but you can go to places as long as they're not your mom's house, right?"

"Yes. I can."

"Okay, we'll ask Senjogahara—she should know the closest restaurant. So, is there any kind of food you like?"

"I like anything as long as it's food."

"Hunh."

"Your hand was delicious too, Mister Araragi."

"My hand isn't food."

"Oh, you don't need to be so modest. It really was delicious."

"………"

She'd probably ingested more than a little of my flesh and blood, so it was no joke.

The cannibal girl.

"By the way, Hachikuji. It's true that you've gone to your mom's home before?"

"It is. I don't tell lies."

"I see…"

But she got lost on her way—and not because it'd been so long. She'd come across the snail, so even if she'd been before—but wait, why did Hachikuji come across that snail in the first place?

A reason.

There was a reason I was attacked by a vampire.

There was one for Hanekawa and Senjogahara, too.

So—there had to be a reason for Hachikuji as well.

"…Hey. I know this is a simple-minded way to look at it, but it's not like your goal is to get to where you're going, it's just to meet your mom, right?"

"It's very insensitive of you to say 'just,' but yes."

"In that case, can't she come and meet you? Even if you can't go to Miss Tsunade's home, it's not as if your mom is locked inside. I'm sure parents have the right to meet their children even after they get divorced—" I was no expert in the field. "Or so I've heard."

"That's impossible. Actually, it's pointless," Hachikuji replied at once. "I would have done that from the beginning if I could. But I can't. I can't even call my mom."

"Hmph…"

"The only thing I can do is visit her like this. Even if I know I'll

186

never get there."

She was saying it in a roundabout way, but did that mean it had something to do with her family situation? It seemed complicated. Then again, I should have guessed as much from the fact that even on Mother's Day, she was having to come all the way to an unfamiliar town by herself. But there had to be a more logical method... For example, Senjogahara could go ahead of us and get to Miss Tsunade's home first... No, a direct strategy like that wouldn't work on an aberration. It wouldn't let us get to where Hachikuji was trying to go, just as it caused Senjogahara's phone to go out of service when she tried to use its GPS. I was able to talk to Oshino on my phone because he and I speaking was fine.

Aberrations—are the world itself.

Unlike living things—they're connected to the world.

Science alone can't shine light on aberrations. Just as people will never stop being attacked by vampires.

There may be no darkness in the world that cannot be illuminated.

But darkness itself will never disappear.

That meant our only option was to wait for Senjogahara to arrive.

"An aberration..." I said. "Though I'm not very clear on the details, to be honest. What about you, Hachikuji? Do you know much about yokai and monsters and that kind of stuff?"

"...Hm?" she paused weirdly before replying, "Oh, no, not at all. Just the *noppera-bo*, I guess."

"Oh, Lafcadio Hearn's faceless monster..."

"Yes, I could really sink my teeth into that story."

"Good for you."

I was sure she could.

Then again, just about anyone in Japan has heard that one.

"Scary, yeah?"

"Yes. But—I don't know any others."

"Right, makes sense."

A yokai, it may have been.

But my case, the vampire—no, it didn't matter.

They were all similar for humans.

It was a conceptual problem.

The deeper part of the problem was—

"Hachikuji—I don't know the details here, but are you really that desperate to see your mom? I honestly don't get why you're willing to go this far."

"I think it's normal for a child to want to see her mother... Am I wrong?"

"No, of course that's true, but..."

Of course that's true. But.

If there was some reason involved that wasn't normal—then I thought we might be able to figure out why Hachikuji had come across the snail. But there didn't seem to be anything definite enough to be called a reason. It was simple, impulsive—a principle akin to nonlinguistic instinct in the edifice of desire.

"Mister Araragi, you live in the same home as both of your parents, don't you? That's why you don't understand. You don't think about what it's like to be lacking something while you're fulfilled. People want what they lack. If you had to live apart from your parents, I'm sure that you'd want to go see them, too."

"Is that how it is?"

That's how it is—I suppose.

A nice problem to have.

—You know, Koyomi, that's why.

"If you don't mind me saying so, Mister Araragi, from where I stand, I'm jealous of the simple fact that you have both of your parents."

"Oh..."

"Jealous as a blue-eyed goblin."

"Oh... You know you got both sides of that kind of wrong."

What would Senjogahara have said in the situation? If she'd heard about Hachikuji's issues, then—no, she probably wouldn't have said a thing. She probably wouldn't have even compared herself to Hachikuji like I was doing. Even if she was in a much closer position to her than I was.

A crab and a snail.

Organisms that lived by the water's edge—was it?

"Judging by your words, Mister Araragi, I get the impression that you aren't very fond of your parents. Is that really the case?"

"Oh, no, it's not like that. It's just—"

Before I continued, the thought crossed my mind that maybe it wasn't something I should be telling a child. Then again, I'd already pried into Hachikuji's circumstances, so even if she was a child, it didn't seem right for me to just trail off.

"You know, I used to be a really good kid," I said.

"It isn't good to lie."

"I'm not lying…"

"I see. Then let's say that it isn't. A little lie never hurt anyone."

"So you're from the village of liars."

"I'm from the village of truth-tellers."

"Is that so. Anyway, while I never spoke in the annoyingly polite way you do, I was a pretty good student and a pretty good athlete, and never got in too much trouble. Also, I never rebelled against my parents for no good reason like the other boys around me. I felt grateful that they were raising me."

"Ahh, how praiseworthy."

"I have two little sisters, too, and they're basically the same. Things were great at home, but then I overdid it when I was trying to get into high school."

"Overdid it?"

"……"

I was impressed by how easily she made our conversation flow.

Was this what they called being a good listener?

"I went and applied to a school for way better students than me—and I managed to get in."

"But that's a wonderful thing. Congratulations."

"No, it wasn't. If I applied for a school that wasn't for me and didn't get in, and that was all, it would have been fine—but as a result, I wasn't able to keep up. You wouldn't believe how bad it gets when you're a washout at a school for smart kids. Not only that, everyone else around me is super serious… People like Senjogahara and I are the exception, not the rule."

189

As for Tsubasa Hanekawa, that embodiment of seriousness, she was an exception just for bothering to deal with a student like me. She had what it took to compensate for it, quite simply.

"And when that happened, I went from being a good kid to the other way around, and just as hard. It's not like there was anything specific that happened to me, though. My father and my mother are the same as ever, and I'm acting the same at home, or at least I feel like I am—but there's just this awkward feeling I can't describe. It comes out no matter what I do, and it lingers. So we all end up worrying too much about each other, and—"

My little sisters.

My two sisters.

—You know, Koyomi, that's why—

"That's why I—never grow up, I've been told. I'm going to stay a child and never become an adult—I've been told."

"So you're a child?" Hachikuji asked. "Then you're the same as me."

"...I don't think so. What they mean is just your frame growing bigger, without getting filled out properly."

"What a rude thing to say to a lady, Mister Araragi. I'll have you know that I'm one of the better-developed students in my class."

"True, your chest was pretty impressive."

"What?! You touched it?! When?!"

Hachikuji's eyes turned to saucers on her astonished face.

"Um...when we were scuffling?"

"That's even more of a shock than the fact you punched me!"

Hachikuji held her head.

She really did seem shocked.

"Wait...it's not like I did it on purpose, and it was only for a split second anyway."

"A split second?! Really? Honestly?!"

"Yeah. I only touched it about three times."

"Not only is that more than a split second, any time past the first has to have been intentional!"

"You're accusing me of something I didn't do. It was an unfortunate accident."

"I've had my first touch stolen from me!"

"Your first touch?"

That's what kids these days talked about?

Grade schoolers really are maturing fast.

"To think that my first touch came before my first kiss... What a naughty girl Mayoi Hachikuji has become!"

"Oh yeah, Hachikuji. Now that you mention it, I realize I forgot to give you the allowance I promised you."

"Please, what a moment to pick to bring that up!"

Next, with her head still in her hands, Hachikuji began to writhe all over as if a wasp had gotten inside her clothes.

The poor thing.

"Come on, don't get yourself so down. It's better than your father taking your first kiss, you know?"

"That sounds like a very normal event!"

"Okay, then it's better than your reflection in a mirror being your first kiss, okay?"

"No girl in our world has had that happen to them!"

Yeah.

You could probably include girls in the next world.

"Grrah!"

Just as I thought Hachikuji was taking her hands off her head, she immediately moved to try to bite my throat. It was where a vampire had bitten me over summer break, so a chill ran down my spine. I somehow managed to get my hands on Hachikuji's shoulders and to push her back, averting any trouble. "Grrarrrarrrarrr!" she gnashed her teeth menacingly. I recalled there being an enemy in some old video game like her (it looked like an iron ball with a chain) as I soothed her.

"N-Now, now. Who's a good girl."

"Please don't treat me like a dog! Or is this your roundabout way of comparing me to a rutting female canine?!"

"Well, if I had to compare you to something, I'd honestly say you're acting more like a rabid one..."

She did have a nice set of teeth, though. She'd bitten into my hand down to the bone, but she hadn't chipped or lost a single one of her teeth, baby or adult. Not only were they perfectly lined, they were unfathomably durable.

"You know, Mister Araragi, you've been acting very brazen for some time now! I don't see a hint of regret on your face! Isn't there something you ought to say after having touched a young girl's delicate chest?!"

"…Thank you?"

"No! I'm demanding an apology from you!"

"You say that, but it happened in the middle of us fighting. How could that be anything short of an act of God? I almost think you should be glad it was just your chest. And like Hanekawa said earlier, you're the one in the wrong for biting someone as ridiculously hard as you did."

"This isn't about who's at fault! Even if I am, I'm in an incredible state of shock! You can't call yourself a grown man if you don't apologize to a girl in shock, even if it's not your fault!"

"Grown men don't apologize," I said in a deep voice. "It cheapens his soul."

"How cool?!"

"Or are you saying you'll never forgive me unless I apologize to you? Saying that you'll forgive someone if they apologize to you…is like admitting you can't be magnanimous toward people who haven't abased themselves."

"Why have I become the one being criticized here? Only a thief could be so bold, as they say… Now you've really gotten me mad… I may be tolerant, but this is like turning both my cheeks inside out!"

"That'd be incredibly tolerant of you…"

"In fact, I won't forgive you even if you apologize!"

"What's the big problem anyway? It's only going to go to waste otherwise."

"And now you're downright defiant, Mister Araragi?! That's not the issue here! And I've only begun puberty, so it's not going to waste!"

"You know, people say they get bigger if you massage them."

"Only men believe that superstition!"

"It's become a sad, boring world out there…"

"Have you been using that superstition as an excuse to squish ladies' breasts all the time? You're disgusting!"

"I've never had the chance, unfortunately."

"So you're a lousy virgin!"

"......"

This elementary school kid knew that expression?

Grade schoolers weren't just maturing fast. They were finished.

I wasn't living in a boring world, but in an awful one...

Then again, I could pretend to lament what was going on in the world today all I wanted, but come to think of it, I'd soaked up that much by the time I was in fifth grade, too. That's how anxiety about younger generations tends to work.

"Grrah! Grarrr! Grarrarrarrr!"

"Ah-wh-h-hey, watch it! Seriously, that's dangerous!"

"A virgin touched me! I'm sullied!"

"How does that part change anything?!"

"I wanted my first to be a smooth operator! But I got you instead, Mister Araragi! My dreams have been crushed!"

"What kind of overblown fantasy is that?! You're making whatever budding feelings of guilt I had disappear, you know!"

"Graarrh! Grrah, graaah, grr!!"

"Oh, just quiet down! You really are a rabid dog! You high-banged, play-biting, no-good woman! Fine, then! I'm gonna squish them so much you'll forget all about your firsts and all about kisses!"

"Eeeek?!"

There he was, a high school boy who was losing it in the face of an elementary school girl, who was threatening to harass her by force, who I'd like to believe wasn't me.

It was me, though...

Fortunately, Mayoi Hachikuji put up far more resistance than I ever could have expected, so this exchange came to an end without having run its course, but rather with my entire body covered in Hachikuji's tooth and scratch marks. After five minutes, an elementary schooler and a high schooler sat silently there on a bench, completely out of breath, drenched in sweat, exhausted.

I was thirsty, but there were no vending machines in the area...

"I'm very sorry..." she said.

"No… I'm the one who should be apologizing."

Mutual apologies were made.

It was a pathetic settlement.

"…Still, Hachikuji. You're used to fights."

"I get into them quite often at school."

"Scuffles like that? Oh, right. You don't pay that much attention to who's a boy and who's a girl when you're in elementary school. But you really know how to get yourself in trouble…"

In spite of her intelligent features.

"You seem to be used to fighting too, Mister Araragi. I suppose battles like that are common once you become a juvenile delinquent?"

"I'm not a delinquent. I'm a washout."

It was the kind of correction that hurt to make.

I was practically wounding myself.

"I'm going to a prep school, so just because I'm a washout doesn't mean I'm a juvenile delinquent. We don't even have a group of delinquents at my school in the first place."

"But in manga, it's standard for student councils of elite high schools to be doing quite wicked things behind the scenes. The smarter someone is, the more malicious of a delinquent they become."

"You can ignore that theory in real life. But anyway, yeah, I do get in a lot of fights with my little sisters."

"Your little sisters, you say. I believe you mentioned earlier that you have two. So are they about my age?"

"No, they're both in middle school. But they might be around your age at heart—both of them act so young."

Though neither of them ever goes so far as to bite me.

One of them practices karate, so there's not much messing around against her.

"You know, they might just get along with you. They're good with kids, or rather, they practically are kids. I'll introduce you to them next time I get a chance."

"Oh… Thank you, but I'll have to pass."

"Okay, then. You know, you're pretty shy for all your good manners. Not that it's important. Well…I guess scuffles, at least, end when one side apologizes to the other."

But today—was a battle of wills.

Still, I thought, it should end with me apologizing.

I knew I should. But still.

"Is something the matter, Mister Ararragi?"

"You added an extra 'r' this time."

"I'm sorry. A slip of the tongue."

"No, I think you did that on purpose."

"A flip by the flung."

"Or maybe not?!"

"I'm sorry, but everyone stumbles over their words from time to time. Or are you trying to say that you've never once had a slip of the tongue?"

"I won't go that far, but I've never messed up saying someone's name before."

"Fine, then say 'She shells she-shells on the she-shore' three times in a row."

"You botched it yourself."

"What do you mean, 'she-shells'?! Are women all you ever think about?"

"You're the one who said that, not me."

"What do you mean, 'she-shore'?! Are women all you ever think about?"

"I don't even understand what that's supposed to mean…"

It was a fun conversation.

"Now that I think about it," I observed, "that's actually pretty hard to say on purpose. She shells, she-shells…"

"Onsha she-shore!"

"…"

Between all the slipping and nipping, her mouth was getting a workout today.

"So. Is something the matter, Mister Araragi?" she asked.

"Nothing's the matter. I'm just feeling a little depressed wondering how I should apologize to my sister."

"Are you going to apologize to her because you squished her chest?"

"I'd never squish my little sister's chest."

"Ah, so you'd squish an elementary school girl's chest, but not your little sister's. I see, so that's where you draw the line."

"Not to be underestimated, eh? That's some sarcasm. What a great illustration of the fact that any situation can be twisted into casting a perfectly innocent man as the villain."

"I don't think I've twisted anything about the situation."

She was right; she'd only explained what had happened. In fact, I was the one who needed to wrestle and twist the context in a quasi-heroic manner to excuse my actions.

"Fine, then I'll put it another way," she offered. "You'd squish an elementary school girl's chest, Mister Araragi, but not a middle school girl's chest."

"Whoever this Mister Araragi you're talking about is, he sounds like one hell of a pedophile. Not someone I'd want to count as a friend."

"You seem to be trying to deny that you're a pedophile."

"You bet."

"I understand that true pedophiles refuse to label themselves as such under any circumstances. They consider innocent young girls to be grownup women and proper peers."

"Thanks for the unwanted factoid…"

Learning useless trivia is nothing more than a waste of brain space.

But more importantly, that wasn't something I wanted to be learning from a grade schooler.

"Either way," she added, "I do think it's dismissible as an act of God in a fight, even if it's your little sister."

"Dammit, don't drag out this topic. Your little sister's chest counts even less as a woman's chest than a grade schooler's. You need to understand that."

"The way of chests. It's very enlightening."

"Don't follow it or anything, I'm begging you. Be that as it may— I got in a little argument when I was leaving home today. Not a scuffle, an argument. And not to rehash what you said earlier, but I feel like I need to apologize even if it's not my fault. If it'll smooth things out. I do—know that. It's what I'm supposed to do."

196

"Yes, it is," Hachikuji nodded with a solemn expression. "My father and my mother were always fighting. Not scuffles, mind you, but arguments."

"And then—they got divorced."

"It may not be my place to say as their only daughter, but I understand they got along very well—at first. I've heard they were madly in love with each other before they married. But—I never once saw them getting along. The two were always fighting."

Even so.

She didn't think they were going to get divorced, she said.

In fact, the idea that they even could had been foreign to Hachikuji—she'd believed that families always stayed together. She must not have known that a practice called divorce existed.

She must not have known.

That her father and her mother could part ways.

"But in terms of what's natural," she said, "that's certainly more natural. They're human, so of course they'd argue and fight. You bite, you're bitten, you love, you hate, that's what comes naturally to us. And so—what they really needed was to work harder if they wanted to stay in love."

"You have to work hard to stay in love? I don't know—I wouldn't call that insincere, but it doesn't feel very sincere to me either. Having to work hard to love something—it's like you're making a conscious effort to make it happen."

"But, Mister Araragi," Hachikuji insisted, "isn't the feeling that we call love a very conscious thing?"

"...Yeah, I guess."

She was right.

Maybe it was—something deserving of work, of effort.

"It's painful to grow bored of something you love, to hate something you love—isn't it? It's dreary, isn't it? If you loved someone ten times over, it's as if you're hating them twenty times over just to hate them as much as you used to love them. That's so—overwhelming."

"Hachikuji," I said, "you do love your mom, don't you."

"Yes, I do. And of course I love my father, too. And I understand how he felt, and I understand that he never wanted things to turn out the way they did. It was difficult for him for a lot of reasons. He was already the breadmaker of the family."

"So your dad baked, too…"

What a guy.

No wonder he had so much on his plate.

"My father and my mother fought, and they split up as a result—but I still love both of them," Hachikuji said.

"Huh… Okay."

"But that's exactly why I feel so uneasy." The way she looked at the ground, I believed her. "My father seems to really hate my mother now—and doesn't seem to have any interest in letting me meet with her. He won't let me call her, and he said I should never see her again."

"………"

"I wonder if I won't forget her some day—if I won't stop loving her some day if we're kept apart like this—and it makes me so uneasy."

That's why.

That's why she came here—all alone.

She didn't have a reason.

She just wanted to see her mother.

"…A snail, huh."

Man.

Why couldn't she be granted her modest wish?

She wasn't asking for much.

Aberration or whatever it was, Lost Cow or whatever it was—why was it getting in Hachikuji's way? Time and time again, at that.

She could never get there.

She was always lost.

…Hm?

Hold on a second, I thought—Oshino had said that this Lost Cow was like what happened with Senjogahara and the crab. The same pattern…what did he mean by that? True, that crab never brought any calamity upon Senjogahara. The results of what it brought upon her were calamitous, but those were just results. In a sense, an essential sense—Senjogahara had only gotten what she wanted.

The crab had granted Senjogahara's wish.

And this was the same pattern… If this were the same formula, only with different variables, what did that mean? What exactly were the implications? If the snail Hachikuji encountered actually wasn't trying to hinder her—

If we were to say it was trying to grant her wish.

What exactly—was the snail doing?

What did Mayoi Hachikuji want?

If I were to look at it that way…didn't it even seem as though Hachikuji had no interest in having this Lost Cow exorcised?

"………"

"Oh? Is something the matter, Mister Araragi? You suddenly started staring at me. Don't you know you're going to make me blush?"

"Um…how do I say this."

"Fall in love with me and you'll get burned."

"…What's, that, supposed, to mean?"

She was making my commas proliferate for no good reason.

"What do you find so confusing? I'm a friend fatale, it's only fitting for me to use cool lines like that."

"Okay, Hachikuji, so it's obvious to me that you meant femme fatale just now, but I don't even know where to take the joke from there. Also, isn't it weird for you to be calling a line about getting burned a 'cool' one?"

"Hmph. You're right. Okay, then." Hachikuji struggled for a moment before rephrasing herself. "Fall in love with me and you'll get a low-temperature burn."

"……"

"That's just lame!"

"And it's still not what you'd call cool."

So she was warm like an electric blanket?

She sounded like a wonderful person.

"Oh, I know what we should do," she said. "We just have to shift our ground. We can keep the line and find a different description for me. While I do wish I could hold on to the cool label, I have no choice but to give it up. Like they say, you can't make an omelet without breaking a few eggs."

"Makes sense. Actually, that might be a pretty standard move, shifting your ground to make your killer line work. Like calling a series 'already popular' on the cover when it's just the second installment. Well, let's try it out. We'll never know otherwise. Okay, so instead of saying you're cool—"

"We'll call me hot."

"Hot-pot Mayoi."

"I still sound like a wonderful person!" Hachikuji lamented exaggeratedly. But as if she'd realized something, she paused and said, "You're trying to change the subject, Mister Araragi!"

So she'd caught on to it.

"We were talking about how you were staring at me, Mister Araragi. What's the matter? Could you have fallen in love with me?"

"……"

She hadn't caught on to it at all.

"While I don't really appreciate being leered at, I will admit that I have very attractive upper arms."

"That would be a unique proclivity."

"Oh? You're saying you don't feel a thing for my upper arms? You do see them, don't you? Their functionary beauty?"

"What, did some bureaucrat decide that they're beautiful?"

Functional, maybe.

"Are you being bashful, Mister Araragi? So you do have a cute side. All right, then, I'll try to understand. I can wait. Please hand out the rain checks."

"Sorry, but I don't have any interest in pipsqueaks."

"Pipsqueak!" Hachikuji looked at me with such shock I thought her eyes might pop out of their sockets. Next, her head started to sway back and forth, like she was having a dizzy spell. "What a terrible insult… That word is so awful I wouldn't be surprised if it were banned from the airwaves some day…"

"I guess it was pretty mean."

"You've wounded me, gravely! I'm developing quite well, I really am! For goodness' sake, Mister Beast Alike!"

"Hey, don't act like it's okay to bring that one up again. That's just as terrible of a thing to call someone, if not worse."

"Fine, then. I'll call you Mister Man Alike instead."

"Now it's like I'm not actually human!"

In fact, calling me that was no laughing matter when I'd been attacked by a vampire and was semi-immortal. The insult stung because it hit way too close to home.

"Oh, that's it. I know what we can do. We just have to look at it a different way, Mister Araragi. We'll come up with neologisms. Society will always try to police what words can and can't be used since people do take offense to them, but there's always the chance that neologisms might be accepted."

"Makes sense. Yeah, you're right. Introducing a new word lets you start off with a fresh slate, so it might not sound as offensive. Like how 'lolicon' doesn't sound quite as bad as 'pedophilia.' All right, let's give it a shot. So we need to come up with brand-new words for pipsqueak you and man-alike me—"

"Urchine and Beastus."

"Whoa, now we sound like a crime-fighting duo!"

"We do! The scales are being peeled from my eyes!"

That sounded painful.

Well, not as painful as listening to us talk, I bet.

"Anyway, I'll take back what I said. But you know, Hachikuji, for a fifth grader, you're pretty well, uh…"

"You're talking about my chest? You're talking about my chest, aren't you?!"

"Just in general. But even so, you still are on a grade-school level. I don't think I'd call you super-elementary."

"Oh. So to your high school eyes, my elementary-school body cuts a slider figure."

"Can't touch them when they break off the plate."

She didn't exactly have curves, either.

Even if she was developing fine, as she said.

She'd meant "slender," by the way.

"…So then, Mister Araragi, why were you looking at me with all that passion in your eyes?"

"Well, you see... Wait, passion?"

"That look you were giving me made my diaphragm go pitter-patter."

"That's called hiccupping."

It was getting hard to keep up with her.

This was turning out to be a test of my stamina as the designated quipper.

"Oh, it's nothing worth worrying about," I said.

"Really. Are you sure?"

"Yeah...I guess."

Was it—the other way around?

Could it be that deep in her heart, contrary to what she was saying—she didn't really want to see her mother? Or perhaps she wanted to but was afraid that her mother would reject her? There was even the possibility that her mother had told her not to come see her—and it seemed like a very real one given what I'd heard so far about Hachikuji's family environment.

If that were the case...things weren't going to be easy.

You wouldn't even have to look at Senjogahara's example to—

"...It smells like another woman here."

Hitagi Senjogahara appeared, completely unannounced.

She'd entered the park still on my mountain bike, displaying her full mastery over it. She was pretty versatile.

"O-Oh... That was quick, Senjogahara."

Her trip back had taken her less than half the time she'd spent to get to Oshino's.

Her entrance was so sudden I didn't have the time to be so much as surprised.

"I made a few wrong turns on my way there," she said.

"Oh, yeah. That cram school can be pretty hard to find. Guess I should've drawn you a map or something."

"And after all of that boasting I did. I feel ashamed."

"I guess you were bragging about your memory or something, weren't you..."

"I've been humiliated at your hands, Araragi... I can't believe you'd get your jollies by disgracing me like this."

"Hold on, I didn't do anything? You only have yourself to blame!"

"So that's what you're into, Araragi. Forcing girls into humiliation roleplay is what excites you. I'll forgive you, though. I can't blame a healthy young man for having those kinds of interests."

"No, that's a pretty unhealthy young man!"

Listening to her, I recalled that Oshino had spoken of a spiritual boundary—a barrier or something—around the cram school. Maybe I really should have been the one to go instead.

But whatever the case, Hitagi Senjogahara was acting awfully brazen for a disgraced woman. Or rather, there was no way she was embarrassed. If anyone was being subjected to humiliation roleplay, it was starting to feel like me...

"I don't mind..." she said. "I can take anything, so long as it's you doing it to me, Araragi..."

"Listen, you need to stick to one personality! You're not adding any more breadth to your character by breaking it entirely! And if you really do care about me, Senjogahara, you need to be warning me as soon as I exhibit such unhealthy traits!"

"Well, I don't actually care about you, Araragi."

"I didn't think so!"

"If it amuses me, then whatever."

"You're being refreshingly honest right now, in fact!"

"And also, Araragi. If we're being honest, then yes, getting lost was part of why it took me so long to get there, but it was also because I had to eat lunch."

"So you did... You always live up to my expectations. Not that it bothers me, that's your own choice, plus it's who you are."

"I ate a lunch for you, too."

"Did you, now... Well, I hope you enjoyed it."

"I did, thank you. It smells like another woman here."

Senjogahara rushed through our pleasantries so that she could drag our conversation back to her very first line.

"Was someone here?" she asked.

"Umm…"

"This scent—Hanekawa?"

"Huh? How are you able to figure that out?" I was honestly astonished. I'd assumed Senjogahara had asked on a lark. "When you say 'scent,' do you mean…like her makeup? But I don't think Hanekawa wears any makeup…"

She was wearing her school uniform, after all. I wouldn't be surprised if you told me chapsticks were off-limits in her mind. When she was in those clothes, at least, she was like a soldier in uniform. Hanekawa would never stray from the school rules in such a flagrant manner, not even by accident.

"I'm talking about the scent of the shampoo she uses. I want to say the only girl in our class who uses that brand is Hanekawa."

"Wait, really? Women can figure that out?"

"To some degree," Senjogahara said in an explanatory tone. "Think of it like your ability to identify a girl by her hips, Araragi."

"I don't remember ever displaying that special ability!"

"Oh? Wait, you can't do that?"

"Stop acting surprised!"

"But you were kind enough to tell me the other day, 'Ah, that nice, seated pelvis and those motherly hips of yours. I bet you'll give birth to a bouncing baby boy, geh heh heh heh!'"

"That's what a dirty old man would say!"

Also, it would take a lot more than that to make me go, "Geh heh heh heh!" And while I'm at it, I thought, I wouldn't describe your hips as motherly.

"So, Hanekawa. She was here."

"……"

Did she realize how much she was scaring me?

I almost wanted to run away.

"I guess she was here," I said. "She already left, though."

"Did you call her here, Araragi? Though now that you mention it, she does live in this area, doesn't she? She'd be good to have around as a guide."

"No, I didn't. She just happened to be passing by. Same as you."

"Hmph. Same as me," Senjogahara repeated. "I guess that's how coincidences are. You never know when they might come in pairs. Did Hanekawa say anything?"

"What do you mean by that?"

"Anything."

"…No, not really. We talked a little…and then she patted Hachikuji on the head and went to the library…no, not the library. But she went somewhere."

"Patted her on the head. Hm—okay… Well, I could see Hanekawa doing that—I suppose?"

"Huh? You mean she likes kids, unlike you?"

"Yes, Hanekawa and I are certainly unlike each other. Yes, we're not the same. We're not the same—so if you'll excuse me for a moment, Araragi," Senjogahara said, before moving her face close to mine. I wondered what she was trying to do at first, until I realized she seemed to be checking what I smelled like. No, it probably wasn't me she was trying to smell—it was probably…

"Hm." She pulled away. "So it looks like there was no love scene between you two."

"…Excuse me? Were you checking if Hanekawa and I were in each other's arms? So you can even detect exactly how strong her scent is… You're incredible, you know that?"

"That wasn't all. Now I know what you smell like, too. I'll at least give you prior warning that from now on, you should act under the assumption that I'm observing your every move."

"I don't know what to say to that, other than I wish you wouldn't…"

But still, what Senjogahara had done was no trivial feat for the average person, so her sense of smell must have been excellent. But hold on, I thought… I'd fought with Hachikuji not once but twice while Senjogahara was gone. Could her scent really have not rubbed off on me? Maybe Senjogahara wasn't bothering to mention it. Maybe the first fight the two of us had in full view of her was throwing her off. Or Hachikuji could have been using an unscented shampoo. Whatever. It didn't seem to matter.

"So, Oshino told you what was going on, right? Hurry up and tell me, Senjogahara. What do we need to do to get her to where she's trying to go?"

To be honest, Oshino's words had stuck with me all this time—I mean the bit about whether or not I'd be lucky enough for missy tsundere (a.k.a. Senjogahara) to come out and tell me.

That is—he'd prefaced.

Which is why I found myself coaxing Senjogahara to give me the full story—Hachikuji was looking up at Senjogahara worriedly, too.

"It's apparently the other way around," Senjogahara divulged. "Araragi. It seems I need to apologize to you—that's what Mister Oshino told me."

"Huh? Oh, wait, have you changed the subject? You really are good at getting off one and onto another. The other way around? You need to apologize to me?"

"To borrow Mister Oshino's words," Senjogahara continued, ignoring my questions. "Say we take a certain fact—and two people observe it according to their points of view and reach different conclusions. In such a case, there's no true way to determine which point of view is the right one—there is no way to prove yourself right in this world."

"……"

"But it's equally wrong to determine that you must be mistaken in that case—according to him. He really does talk like he sees through everything, doesn't he?"

I hate it, she said.

"Wait… What are you talking about, Senjogahara? Well, not you, but Oshino? How does that apply to our situation here—"

"He says it's very simple to be freed of the snail—the Lost Cow. Explaining it in words would be very simple. This is what Mister Oshino told me—you'll be lost as long as you follow the snail, and you won't be lost if you distance yourself from it."

"You follow it—and that's why you get lost?"

What was that supposed to mean? It was so simple it didn't make sense. Like he had left some words out. In fact, they seemed somewhat off the mark for him. I looked at Hachikuji, but she wasn't reacting. Senjogahara's words did seem to be having some sort of effect on her, though—her lips were shut.

She said nothing.

"In other words, there's no need for an exorcism or for prayer. No one's been possessed, and no one's being harmed—apparently. That much is the same as what happened with me and that crab. And what's more—with the snail, the targeted person is actually *approaching* the aberration. Not unconsciously or subconsciously, either. Entirely of their own volition. They're just going along with the snail. They're choosing to follow after it because that's what they want. And that's why they get lost. Which is why you need to distance yourself from the snail, Araragi—that's all that needs to happen."

"Hold on, we're not talking about me here. We're talking about Hachikuji. Anyway, in that case—how does that make any sense? It's not like Hachikuji wants to follow this snail around—how could that possibly be what she's trying to do?"

"That's what I'm trying to say. Apparently—it's the other way around."

The tone of Senjogahara's voice was no different from usual, her same old flat one. You couldn't read any emotions at all from it.

She was no actor.

But—she seemed to be in a bad mood.

A very bad mood.

"Apparently," she continued, "the aberration known as the Lost Cow doesn't make you lose your way to your destination. You lose it on the way back."

"O-On the way back?"

"It doesn't keep you from getting there, it keeps you from returning—according to him."

It wasn't about going—but about coming back?

Coming back… Come back where?

To your own home?

Visiting and—arriving?

"Okay, fine," I said. "But—so what? I get what you're trying to say. S-Still—Hachikuji's home… It's not as if she's trying to return there, is it? She's clearly trying to get to her destination, Miss Tsunade's home—"

"That's why—I need to apologize to you, Araragi. I do, I know I do, but please, let me explain. I wasn't doing it out of malice...or even intentionally. I was sure that *I was the one* who was mistaken."

"......"

I didn't understand what she was trying to say—but.

I could tell—it felt pregnant with meaning.

"How could I not be? There was something strange about me for more than two years. It was only last week that I finally became normal again. So if something happened—I couldn't help but think that I was the one who was mistaken."

"Hey...Senjogahara."

"It was like me and the crab—the Lost Cow can only be seen by someone who has a reason to. Which is why it presented itself to you, Araragi."

"...No, like I've been saying, the snail didn't present itself to me, but Hachikuji—"

"Yes. Hachikuji."

"......"

"Araragi, this is what I'm trying to say. You felt awkward because it was Mother's Day, you fought with your little sisters, and you don't want to go home. So that girl over there, Hachikuji?"

Senjogahara pointed at Hachikuji.

Or at least, she must have meant to—

Her direction was totally off.

"I can't see her."

I was startled—and my eyes hurried over to get a look at Hachikuji.

The little girl with intelligent features.

With bangs so short her eyebrows were showing, with her hair in pigtails.

Seeing her, carrying that large backpack—

She somehow resembled a snail.

0 0 7

Once upon a time, long long ago—would take you too far into the past, this was about ten years back. There was once a married couple whose relationship reached an end. A husband and a wife. Together they were a pair. A pair that was the envy of all around them, a pair that everyone was sure would be happy, but in the end, their matrimonial relation was a short-lived thing lasting less than ten years.

I don't think it's a question of right or wrong.

That was normal, too.

It was even normal for that couple to have had an only daughter—and after a dismal little back and forth, it was decided that the girl's father would be the one to look after her.

The marriage was a quagmire by its last days. It didn't end so much as it collapsed, to the point that you were afraid it might have turned bloody had the couple lived under the same roof for even one more year—and the father made the mother vow never to see their only daughter again.

The agreement had nothing to do with the law.

She was half-forced into the vow.

But their only daughter wondered.

Was her mother really forced into it?

The daughter, whose father made her vow likewise that she would never see her mother again, wondered—did her mother, who had loved her father so much, but who now hated him so much, hate her too? How could her mother make such a vow otherwise—if she was half-forced into it, what about the other half? But the daughter could say the same of herself.

She had made a similar vow to never see her mother again.

Right.

Just because it was her mother.

Just because it was her only daughter.

Eternity was not a quality of any relationship.

Whether forced or not, a vow can't be taken back once made. Only the shameless spoke of the fruits of their own decisions in the passive, and not active, voice—the daughter had been raised in this manner by none other than her mother.

Her father took custody of her.

She was made to abandon her mother's surname.

But—even such thoughts fade.

With time, even such sorrows fade.

Because time is a thing that is kind to us all alike.

So kind it can be cruel.

Time passed, and the nine-year-old only daughter was eleven.

She was stunned.

She couldn't remember her mother's face—no, it wouldn't be accurate to say that. The girl could picture it vividly. But—she was no longer sure whether the face she remembered was her mother's.

It was the same even with photographs.

The pictures of her mother that her father secretly kept with him—she could no longer tell if the woman in them was her mother.

Time.

All thoughts fade.

All thoughts deteriorate.

Which is why—

The daughter decided to go meet her mother.

On the second Sunday of that May.

On Mother's Day.

There was no way she could tell her father, of course not, nor could

210

she tell her mother about it in advance. The daughter had no idea how her mother was faring—and also.

If she hated her?

If she saw her as a nuisance?

Or—if she'd forgotten her?

It would be such a shock.

So that she could turn back and go home at any time, so that the option to abort her plan would be available to her until the very end, the daughter kept the trip a secret from everyone, even her closest friends, to be honest—and visited her mother.

Tried to visit her mother.

She fixed her hair herself and stuffed her favorite backpack full of old memories, ones that would surely delight her mother. To avoid getting lost, gripped in the daughter's hand was a note with her mother's address written on it.

But.

The only daughter never made it there.

She never made it to her mother's home.

But why?

But why?

But really, why?

She was so sure the light was green—

"—And that only daughter was me."

So acknowledged—Mayoi Hachikuji.

No, maybe it was more like a confession.

It was hard for me to see it as anything else when I saw her repentant face, teetering on the verge of tears.

I looked at Senjogahara.

Her expression was unchanged.

She really—never showed how she felt.

She couldn't possibly not be having thoughts of her own, though, in this situation.

"And so…" I asked, "you've been lost ever since?"

Hachikuji didn't reply.

She didn't even try to look in my direction.

Senjogahara spoke up. "That which couldn't reach its destination keeping others from returning home—Mister Oshino wouldn't confirm it, but for our amateur understanding, it might be like a residual haunting. The way there, and the way home—the journey and the return. A pilgrim's path from point to point. In other words, Hachikuji, the eighty-nine temples—that's what he said."

The Lost Cow.

That's why it was lost itself—and not the misleading cow.

The reason why it had to be that way.

Right, the aberration itself—was lost.

"But—a snail?"

"Come on," Senjogahara chided. Coolly. "The metamorphosis into a snail—must be posthumous. Mister Oshino didn't call it a residual haunting, but he did use the word 'ghost.' Couldn't that be what he meant?"

"But—that..."

"But that's exactly why—this isn't like a regular ghost. It doesn't follow the pattern of ghosts as we generally think and conceive of them. It must be different from the crab too..."

"That..."

That was true, though... Just as it didn't have to be a cow despite having that name, it didn't necessarily take the form of a snail simply because it was called a snail. I'd misapprehended—the essence of what an aberration is.

Names give shape to nature.

The body of it.

Seeing shouldn't necessarily be believing—and on the flip side, not seeing isn't necessarily counterfactual, Araragi—

Mayoi Hachikuji.

Lost Hachikuji.

Mayoi—a word originally used to describe the warp and weft fraying and tangling. That's why, in addition to meaning "lost," it refers to attachments that keep dead spirits from resting in peace. Moreover, while the character "yoi" on its own means the time around dusk, that is to say twilight, the hour when you encounter the weird, the character "ma," which usually means "true," acts as a negative prefix in this instance, so that the archaic term "mayoi" signifies the middle of the night, two in the morning to be precise—yes, the so-called dead of night. Sometimes a cow, sometimes a snail, sometimes humanoid—but, come on, really, just as Oshino said—

That would be too obvious—wouldn't it.

"Umm…are you actually telling me that you can't see Hachikuji? Look, she's right here—"

I wrapped an arm around Hachikuji's shoulders as the girl hung her head and, practically lifting her, pointed her toward Senjogahara. Mayoi Hachikuji. She was right there—I was touching her. I could feel her warmth, her softness. I could even see her shadow on the ground. It hurt when she bit me, and—

It was fun when we chatted.

"I can't see her," Senjogahara insisted. "I can't hear her, either."

"But you were acting like you—"

Wait—no.

I was wrong.

Senjogahara had told me from the start.

—I can't even see it.

"All I saw was you mumbling to yourself in front of that sign before miming out a crazed fight—I had no clue what you were doing. But according to you—"

According to me.

That was it. I'd conveyed all of it to Senjogahara—in every instance. Ah, of course—that's why, that's why Senjogahara—never took the note with the address on it.

Forget taking it, she saw nothing.

There was nothing.

"But—" I objected, "if you'd just told me that to begin with—"

"Like I said, how could I? I couldn't. When something like that happens—if I can't see what you see, it's only normal for me to assume that I'm the funny one for not seeing it."

"………"

For more than two years.

Hitagi Senjogahara had to live with an aberration.

—I'm the funny one, the abnormal one.

The mentality was hammered into her with a scale-busting ferocity. After you come across an aberration, even once, you carry that burden with you for the rest of your life. To a greater or lesser degree—if I had to say which, then greater. Once you learn that these things exist in the world, no matter how powerless, you can't feign ignorance.

That was why.

Yet Senjogahara, who'd been freed from her problem at last, didn't want to think that something had gone wrong with her again, and not wanting to think that something was wrong with her, nor wanting me to think so—she acted like she could see Hachikuji when she couldn't.

She went along with me.

Ah ha…

That was why Senjogahara seemed to be turning a blind eye to Hachikuji… The words "blind eye" were almost stupidly apt. And Hachikuji must have been acting that way…hiding behind my legs as if she were trying to avoid Senjogahara—for the same reason.

They hadn't said a word to each other.

Senjogahara and Hachikuji.

"Senjogahara… That's why you said you'd go meet Oshino—"

"I wanted to ask him. I wanted to ask him what was going on. But he chastised me when I did—or actually, he was appalled. No, he might have even laughed at me."

I could see why. What a silly little situation. It was like a joke.

So ridiculous it wasn't funny.

"So the one who'd come across the snail—was me."

First a demon—and then a snail.

Oshino, too—he'd told me from the very beginning.

"Child aberrations," Senjogahara continued, "little girls, in particular—are apparently quite common. I already knew that to some degree, of course. They're even in our Japanese-class textbooks. A ghost in a kimono who causes travelers to lose their way in the mountains, a girl who sneaks in among children who're playing and snatches one of them near the end—though I wasn't well-versed enough to have heard of the

Lost Cow. You know, Araragi, this is what Mister Oshino told me. For you to meet one—you have to wish not to go home. Well, it's a little passive to be called a 'wish,' but we've all thought that before. We all have family issues."

"...Ah!"

Tsubasa Hanekawa.

It was the same for her.

Her home was a troubled, warped one—so she went out for walks on Sundays.

Just like me, or maybe even more.

And so Hanekawa—could see Hachikuji, too.

She saw her, touched her—and spoke to her.

"An aberration..." I muttered, "that grants a wish."

"It sounds nice when you put it that way, but you could also say it's taking advantage of a person's weakness. It's not like you really don't want to go back home, Araragi. So maybe we shouldn't say a passive wish, but a certain reason."

"......"

"But Araragi, that's exactly why it's so easy to deal with a Lost Cow. Remember what I said in the beginning? Don't follow it. Distance yourself. That's all you need to do."

Wishing—to lose your way.

That was true—it made sense. Following around a snail whose destination eluded it for all eternity was a sure way never to come home.

Put into words—it was very simple.

Hanekawa was able to stroll out of the park.

Likewise, going home was all it took to go home.

You couldn't if you followed a thing that went on and on.

But.

Not wanting to come home? In the end, it's the only place a human being can return to.

"It's not a particularly malicious aberration, nor a particularly powerful one. It usually isn't all that harmful. That's what he told me. A Lost Cow is a prank—a small bit of mystery, nothing more. So—"

"So?" I interrupted her.

I couldn't bear to listen—not anymore.

"So what, Senjogahara?"

"……"

"That's not it, and you know it isn't. That's not it at all, Senjogahara—I get what you're saying, and sure, this is a neat little explanation for all those things that were nagging at me this whole time—but you know that's not what I wanted to ask Oshino. Thanks for the etymological erudition, but it wasn't for such a lesson that I asked you to go to him."

"…Then what was it for?"

"Come on!"

Clench.

My hand clamped down harder on Hachikuji's shoulder.

"What I wanted to ask him was—how to bring her, Hachikuji, to her mother—that was it, remember? That was all, from the beginning. Who am I supposed to impress with all that minutiae? Useless trivia— is nothing more than a waste of brain space. That's not what matters here—and you know it."

It wasn't about Koyomi Araragi.

It was about Mayoi Hachikuji, and no one else.

I just had to distance myself from her? No.

That was what I shouldn't do.

"…Don't you get it, Araragi? That girl—isn't really there. She's not there, nor anywhere else. Hachikuji…Mayoi Hachikuji, was it? The girl…is already dead. She's not meant to be—she hasn't been possessed by an aberration, she, herself, is the aberration—"

"So what?!" I yelled.

I yelled—at Senjogahara.

"Not meant to be? Then who is?!"

"……"

Not me, not you—and not Tsubasa Hanekawa.

Nothing—lasts forever.

Even then.

"M-Mister Araragi? That hurts."

Hachikuji squirmed helplessly under my arm. I hadn't realized that

I was holding her too tight, and she seemed to be in pain from my fingernails digging into her shoulder.

She seemed to be in pain.

She continued.

"U-Um, Mister Araragi. The lady, Miss Senjogahara, is right. I-I'm—"

"Shut up!"

No matter what she said—her words didn't reach Senjogahara.

They only reached me.

But in that voice that only I could hear, she'd announced honestly from the beginning—that she was a lost snail.

She'd done her best to announce it.

She'd also said—

The very first thing she said.

"You couldn't hear her, Senjogahara—so I'll repeat it for you. You wouldn't believe the very first thing she said—to me, and to Hanekawa, out of what seemed like nowhere—"

Please don't speak to me.

I don't like you.

"Do you get it, Senjogahara? Having to say that line to every single person she meets because she doesn't want anyone to follow her—do you understand how she must feel? Someone who has to bite any hand that pats her head? Because I can't."

You should ask people for help—cruel words.

She was it, herself.

She was the funny one.

How could she bring herself to say that?

"But even if we don't understand, feeling like you have to say such things even though you've lost your way, even though you're all alone—haven't both of us gone through that in a different form? We might not have felt the same, but we felt the same pain. I came into an immortal body—and yours was burdened with an aberration, too. Isn't that so? Isn't that the truth? Then whatever it is, a lost cow or a snail—if that's what she, herself, is, that changes everything. I know you can't see her, hear her, or even smell her—but that's exactly why bringing her to her mother's side—falls on me."

"…I thought you might say that."

I started to calm down after my entirely misdirected outburst, and of course I knew that what I was proposing was ridiculous—but Senjogahara responded without her complexion changing a shade or a single twitch of an eyebrow.

"Finally—I'm getting you, Araragi."

"…What?"

"It looks like I was mistaken about you. No, not mistaken. I had a creeping, or maybe nagging feeling about it—I guess you could say I'm no longer under any illusions. Araragi, hey Araragi. Last Monday, thanks to a slight misstep on my part, you found out about the problem I'd been living with… And that day, that very same day—you reached out to me, yes?"

I might be able to help you out.

I reached out to her, saying so.

"Honestly," Senjogahara said, "I've been having trouble figuring out what your action signifies—why would you ever do that? It's not like you'd get anything out of it. You had nothing to gain from saving me— so why? Could it have been that you saved me because it was me?"

"……"

"But that wasn't it. It seems not to be. Instead, it's simply that… you'd save anyone, Araragi."

"Save? I wouldn't go that far. You're exaggerating, anyone would do what I did in that situation—and you said it yourself, I just happened to have a similar problem, just happened to know Oshino—"

"Even if you hadn't had a similar problem or known Mister Oshino, you would have done what you did—right? It sounds that way from what he told me."

What did that bastard tell her?

A bunch of lies peppered with half-truths, I was sure.

"At the very least—" she continued, "I wouldn't think to speak to a grade schooler I'd never met just because I'd seen her standing in front of a residential map twice."

"……"

"When you're by yourself for long enough, you start to think that maybe you're special. After all, when you're on your own, you aren't merely 'one of them.' But it's because you can't be, that's all. What a joke. Plenty of people actually noticed my problem in the two-plus years after I came across the aberration—but whatever the end result, the only one who was anything like you, Araragi, was you."

"...Well, sure, I'm the only person who's me."

"Yes. Exactly."

Senjogahara smiled.

Then, although it must have been a stroke of luck that the angle was right—Hitagi Senjogahara stared straight at Mayoi Hachikuji.

"Araragi, I have one last message for you from Mister Oshino. He said, 'I bet Araragi is going to spout starry-eyed nonsense, so being the kind, kind person that I am, I'm handing down a little trick that ought to work just this time.'"

"A little...trick?"

"Really—like he sees through it all. I don't have the slightest idea what that man thinks he's doing with his life."

Okay, let's go, Senjogahara said, straddling my mountain bike with ease. With practiced ease, like the machine was already her property.

"Go? Go where?"

"To Miss Tsunade's home, of course. Being good Samaritans, we're taking Hachikuji there. I'll lead the way, so follow after me. Also, Araragi?"

"What now?"

"*I love you*," she said in English.

"........."

Pointing at me, in the same tone as ever.

........., I thought for a few more seconds, before realizing that I seemed to have become the very first man in Japan whose classmate confessed her love for him in English.

"Congratulations," Hachikuji said.

The word was out of place and off the mark in every possible sense.

0 0 8

Then, an hour later, Senjogahara, Hachikuji, and I got there—the place where, ten or so years ago (I don't know exactly how many, but around there), the living human girl Mayoi Hachikuji tried to go on Mother's Day—to the precise address written on the note.

It took some time.

Still—it was easy.

"...But, this—"

Yet—there was no sense of accomplishment.

Absolutely no sense of accomplishment given the sight in front of us.

"Senjogahara—are you sure this is the place?"

"Yes. I'm sure of it."

There seemed to be no room to argue with her statement of fact.

Hachikuji's mother's home—the Tsunade family home.

It was a clean, flat—plot of land.

Surrounded by a fence, with a sign thrust into its bare earth—private property, no trespassing.

Judging by the rust on the edges of the sign, it seemed to have been in that state for a long time now.

Residential development.

Town planning.

It wasn't quite a road, like Senjogahara's home had become—but like hers, not a trace of it had been left behind.

"…Is this seriously happening?"

The one-time trick that homebody Mèmè Oshino had proposed was so utterly plain and simple that hearing it made you think, Oh, of course. The Lost Cow may have existed as a snail, but if it was a ghostly aberration, then it couldn't accumulate essential new information as memories—supposedly.

Basically, these kinds of aberrations don't exist.

Existences who don't exist as existences.

If there is no one to see it, it isn't there.

To apply that to what transpired that day, the exact moment I happened to sit down on the bench and glance at the map—was when Hachikuji presented herself, came into existence—supposedly.

Likewise, as far as Hanekawa was concerned, the exact moment she happened to pass through the park and glance at the spot next to where I was sitting—was when Hachikuji presented herself, logically speaking. Presenting itself the very moment it's witnessed, rather than leading a sustained existence as an aberration—in that sense, with the Lost Cow, "encounter" is only half-accurate a term.

Being there only when it's seen—the observer and the observed. I'm sure Hanekawa would have displayed her scientific knowledge unabashedly with an appropriate metaphor, but I couldn't come up with a good simile, and while Senjogahara must have known one, she wasn't going out of her way to tell me.

Anyway.

Information stored as memories—in other words, knowledge.

Not to mention me, who didn't know the area, the snail was able to cause Senjogahara, who was only accompanying me and who didn't even see it, to lose her way—and it was also able to block cell phone signals. As a result—the target would continue to be lost forever.

But.

What it didn't know—it didn't know.

In fact, even if it did know, it couldn't react accordingly.

Take, for example, town planning.

The neighborhood looked nothing like it did a year ago, let alone ten years ago—so if you didn't take a shortcut, didn't make any detours, and of course didn't head straight there—

If you used a route made up of only new roads—a modest aberration like the Lost Cow couldn't do anything about it.

An aberration is unlikely to gain in years—a girl aberration always stays a girl—supposedly.

It will never become an adult—

Just like me.

Hachikuji was in fifth grade ten years ago…so rearranging the timeline would make Mayoi Hachikuji older than both me and Senjogahara. Yet she spoke of getting up to no good at school like it was only yesterday, and incremental memories in the usual sense didn't exist for her.

Didn't—

Exist.

And so—and so.

New wine in an old wineskin—that's what he'd said, apparently.

Oshino, that damned annoying fellow, truly sees through things—even though he hasn't beheld Hachikuji in person or heard her circumstances in detail—barely knowing anything about this town, at that, he goes off and acts like he knows it all.

But in terms of results, it was a success.

Picking streets with dark, black asphalt that had to be new, like we were following a treasure map, avoiding old or merely repaved streets as much as possible—along the way, taking that street, too, where Senjogahara's home used to stand—after an hour of this.

Under normal circumstances, it was less than a ten-minute walk from the park, probably less than a third of a mile as the bird flies, but after over an hour—

We reached our destination.

We reached it, but.

What we found—was a clean plot of land.

"Guess you can't expect everything to fall into place…" I muttered.

Right.

How could it—given how much the town and its streets had changed, our destination couldn't be the one thing that hadn't. In less than a year, even Senjogahara's home had become a road. We wouldn't have been able to put the stratagem into practice in the first place if there hadn't been new roads around our destination. There was a strong chance that the destination had changed, too; it was implicit from the start—still, not even that much falling into place would spoil everything, wouldn't it? That would make it all pointless, no? If that part was a bust, for goodness' sake, so was the whole plan.

Is the world such a hard place?

Do dreams just not come true?

If the very place the Lost Cow was trying to go was gone—then she really was a lost snail, forever lost, forever drifting, spiraling around and around with no end in sight—no?

What a calamity.

Oshino.

Had that psychedelic Hawaiian shirt-wearing asshole seen through this conclusion—this ending, too? Was that why—in fact, precisely why he deliberately…

As frivolous, flippant, and talkative as Mèmè Oshino was—he never said goodbye, and he never answered a question that he wasn't asked. He didn't act unless he was requested to, and even then, there was no guarantee he'd agree to it.

He was totally fine not saying what needed to be said.

"Wa-ah—"

I could hear Hachikuji wailing next to me.

I'd been so busy feeling mugged by reality that I wasn't attending to Hachikuji, the heart of this matter, and now belatedly turned to her—

She was crying.

But she wasn't looking down—her face was turned forward.

Looking toward the plot of land—where her home must have been.

"Wa-a-a-ah—"

And then.

She dashed past me and ran.

"—I'm back! I'm home!"

Oshino.

Naturally, he must have seen this conclusion coming—seen through to this ending, as a matter of course.

He was a man—who didn't say what needed to be said.

I really wished he'd told me from the beginning.

What Hachikuji would see once she was there.

What kind of scenery this place—a mere plot of land to my eyes and Senjogahara's and no doubt nothing like it used to look—would show the Lost Cow, Mayoi Hachikuji.

How it might present itself.

Neither development nor planning was—relevant.

Not even time.

Soon, the figure of the girl carrying the large backpack began to—grow dim, blurry, and slight…and before I knew it, I couldn't see her.

Gone from my sight.

Gone.

But the girl had said, "I'm back." It was the home of the family of her divorced mother, and in no way the girl's now, just a destination that she was destined for—yet the kid had said, "I'm back."

Like she'd come home.

And to me.

That sounded wonderful.

Nothing short of wonderful.

"…Good work, Araragi. You looked halfway cool there," Senjogahara said after a while.

In a voice rather devoid of emotion.

"I didn't do anything, really," I pointed out. "If anything, you were the one who did all the work this time around, not me. Even that trick wouldn't have stood muster as a method without someone like you who knows the area."

"That's true—that may be true, but it's not what I'm talking about, okay? I will say that I was surprised that it was an empty plot, though. Her only daughter got into a traffic accident on the way to visit her—and the fact was so unbearable the whole family moved, I assume. Of course, I'm sure you could come up with lots of other reasons if you wanted to."

"Sure—I mean, if you're going to go there, we don't even know whether Hachikuji's mother is still alive."

Moreover—the same went for her father.

Maybe, I wondered—Hanekawa actually knew. She seemed to have some idea when I asked her about the Tsunade family. If particular circumstances had made them move away—and she knew what they were, she'd definitely keep mum. That was the kind of person Hanekawa was. To say the least—she wasn't actually a stickler for the rules.

She was just fair.

Either way, the case was closed, then...

Now that it was over, it felt so sudden. And I noticed that the sun—was already setting on this Sunday. It was mid-May, and the days were still short...which meant I needed to be going back home.

Just like Hachikuji.

Right. It was my turn to make dinner, too.

"Okay, then, Senjogahara... Let's go back to get my bike."

Senjogahara had attempted to lead me and Hachikuji while riding my mountain bike, but it didn't take long for her to see, without being told, that a mountain bike was pointless when she had to keep pace with walkers and worthless once it turned into a piece of rolling luggage. We ended up leaving it back in the parking lot.

"Oh. By the way, Araragi."

Senjogahara stood still—and continued to face the plot as she spoke.

"You still haven't given me your reply."

"......"

My reply...

I was pretty sure what she was talking about.

"Um. Senjogahara. About that—"

"I should tell you this up front, Araragi. You know those romantic comedies where it's obvious the two characters are going to get together at the end, but instead they drag out the story with a bunch of lukewarm twists and turns while they're more than friends but not quite lovers? I hate those."

"...Do you."

"If you want me to elaborate, I also hate sports manga that spend roughly a year on every match when you know they're going to win the championship anyway, and I also hate action manga where they spend forever fighting underlings when it's clear they're going to beat the last boss and bring peace to the world."

"You've just crossed out every single manga written for anyone under sixteen."

"What're you going to do, then?"

She was pressing me for an answer without giving me any time to think.

Giving an evasive reply was not an option, at all. If a girl brought all of her friends to confess her love to a boy, he wouldn't feel nearly as suffocated.

"No, Senjogahara, I think you've gotten something mixed up. Or it's a little hasty. Yes, I did contribute in no small way to solving your problem last Monday, but um, if you don't separate your indebtedness, for lack of a better word, from those other feelings, then—"

"Could you be thinking of the idiotic law that people fall prey to love more readily in a crisis, which makes complete light of human reason and utterly fails to take into account the thorny situation two friends are put in when their true natures are thereby revealed?"

"Idiotic—well, yes, I guess? I do think you'd be stupid to confess your love on a shaky suspension bridge, but...see, you were talking about wanting to pay me back. I felt the same way then, too—please don't feel more indebted to me than...or actually, whatever the situation or background, I don't want to be calling in a debt and taking advantage of someone."

"That was just an excuse on my part. I only acted that way because I wanted to hand you the initiative and allow you to be the one to confess to me. You let a valuable opportunity get away from you, you foolish man. You've wasted the one and only time I'm ever propping up another human being."

"………"

What a way to put it.

So that's what she was going for, after all…

It was an invitation…

"Don't worry, Araragi. I don't really feel that indebted to you."

"…Is that so."

Whaaat.

I didn't know about that, either.

"Because, Araragi, you'd save anyone."

Though I wasn't completely certain of that this morning, she continued on an even keel.

"It wasn't because I'm me—but I prefer it that way. Even if it wasn't me whom you were saving—if I'd watched you saving Hanekawa, for example, I think I'd still find you special. I wasn't special, but becoming special for someone like you would be thrilling. Well…I think I'm exaggerating a bit, but I guess I could admit that I just have fun talking with you, Araragi."

"…But it's not as if—we've talked that much."

That was an understatement.

It was easy to overlook the fact because of just how much concentrated time we'd spent together last Monday, Tuesday, and today, but the only times she and I had ever spoken to each other this much—were that Monday, that Tuesday, and today.

Three days, no more.

We might've been in the same class for three years, but—

We were practically strangers.

"Right," Senjogahara nodded in full agreement. "Which is why I want us to talk more."

To spend more time together.

To get to know.

To get to love.

"I don't think it's anything as cheap as love at first sight," she said. "But I'm not so patient a person as to want to spend time lining everything up. How do I put it—yes, maybe it's that I want to make the effort and get to love you."

"…I see."

When she put it that way—it sounded right.

There was nothing I could say in reply.

You had to work hard to stay in love—because the feeling we call love is a very conscious thing. In that case—maybe what Senjogahara was saying was fine.

"Anyway," she noted, "I think these things are a question of timing to begin with. I would've been fine with us staying friends, but at the end of the day, I'm greedy. I settle for nothing but extremes."

Just think of it as having gotten mixed up with a foul woman.

Those were her words.

"You've ended up in this situation because you're kind to everyone you meet, Araragi. Take it to heart, you reap what you sow. But don't worry, even I can tell the difference between feeling indebted and those other emotions. After all, this past week—I've been able to come up with all kinds of fantasies involving you."

"Fantasies…"

"What a satisfying week it was."

Really—she was so direct about this stuff.

What did I do in those fantasies, I wondered, and what was done to me?

"You know, just think of it this way," she added. "In a dismal turn, you caught the eye of a love-starved psycho virgin who falls for anyone who shows her the slightest bit of kindness."

"…Okay, then."

"It wasn't your day. Curse the way you've led your life."

So—she was even prepared to degrade herself.

And there I was, forcing her to go that far.

That far.

…God, I was being lame.

I was so small.

"So, Araragi. I know I've said a lot, but."

"What is it."

"If you turn me down, I'm going to kill you and go on the run."

"That's just murder! At least make it a lovers' suicide!"

"That's just how serious I am about this."

"…Phew. Is that a fact."

I let out a contemplative sigh from somewhere deep inside me.

Oh boy.

What an interesting woman.

In the same class for three years, and yet only three days—what a waste. What an absurd, extravagant amount of time Koyomi Araragi had frittered away.

When I caught her that day.

What a good thing it was me.

What a good thing it was—that Hitagi Senjogahara had been caught by Koyomi Araragi.

"If you sputter feeble words like needing some time to think about it, Araragi, I'm going to look down on you. You can embarrass a woman only so much, you know."

"I know… I already think I'm being pretty pathetic right now. But can I give you just one condition, Senjogahara?"

"What might it be? Do you want to watch me shave my body hair for a week or something?"

"Out of all the things that have come out of your mouth until now, that is unmistakably one of the worst!"

Unmistakably, both in terms of content and timing.

I paused for a few seconds, then faced Senjogahara. "I guess you could call it more of a promise than a condition—"

"A promise… What might it be?"

"Senjogahara, you've acted like you can see things that you can't see, and like you can't see things that you can see—and I don't want you doing any more of that. No more, okay? If you think something is strange, come out and say that it's strange. Stop trying to be considerate about it. We've experienced what we've experienced, we know what we know, and I'm sure the both of us are going to bear that burden for the rest of our lives—because we've learned that these things exist. So if our opinions ever clash, I want us to talk about it. Promise me."

"No problem."

Senjogahara's expression was cool—unchanging as always, but in her seemingly rash, even thoughtless, yet absolutely instant reply, my heart found something, however small it was, to latch onto.

So, you reap what you sow.

Usually, the way you've led your life.

"Okay, let's go," I said. "It's already gotten dark out, and, uhm…I'll give you a ride home? Is that what you'd say here?"

"There's no way two people can ride on that bicycle."

"Three might not be able to, but two can. It's got one of those rods."

"Rods?"

"To put your feet on. I don't know their official name, but…you put it on your back wheel, and you can stand on it. You just have to hold onto the shoulders of whoever's riding. We can play rock-paper-scissors to figure out who's in front. That snail isn't here anymore, so we can just go home like normal. Not that I remember the complicated route we followed to get here, anyway… Okay, Senjogahara, let's—"

"Wait, Araragi."

Senjogahara still stood there.

She stood still and grabbed my wrist.

Hitagi Senjogahara, who had denied herself physical contact for so long—naturally, it was the first time she'd ever touched me like that.

Touching.

Seeing.

It meant that we're here.

To each other.

"Do you think you could say it out loud for me?"

"Out loud?"

"I don't like silent partnerships."

"Ah—got it."

I gave it some thought.

It seemed unrefined to reply in kind with English, not to this woman who wanted nothing but extremes. Then again, I had only a surface knowledge of other languages, which in any case wouldn't be any more original.

Which left—

"I hope it catches on."

"Excuse me?"

"My heart smelts for you, Senjogahara."

So by the by, and all in all.

Hanekawa's single-minded delusion had come true to a tee. She really did know everything after all.

009

The epilogue, or maybe, the punch line of this story.

The next day, I was roused from bed as usual by my little sisters Karen and Tsukihi. The fact that they were doing this seemed to indicate that my apology, essentially a statement of unconditional surrender, had worked, safely dissipating their anger. That, or maybe it was my promise that while I couldn't do anything for Mother's Day this year, I would under no circumstances leave the confines of our home next year. Either way, it was Monday. Nothing eventful about it, as supreme a weekday as you could get. I had a light breakfast and headed to school. Not on my mountain bike, but on my granny bike. When I thought that today was the day Senjogahara would return to school, my legs felt lighter as they turned the pedals. But as I was on my way down a slope not too far from home, I nearly collided with a girl waddling around the street and hastily hit the brakes.

Bangs so short her eyebrows were showing, her hair in pigtails.

The girl who stood there carried a large backpack.

"Ah…Mister Aarragi."

"You switched two letters around."

"I'm sorry. A slip of the tongue."

"What're you doing here?"

"Oh, well, I'm…"

The kind of confused expression you might see on a ninja whose attempt at stealth had failed crossed her face before she showed an embarrassed smile.

"Well, actually! Thanks to you, Mister Araragi, I've gone from being a residual ghost to a wandering one! A posthumous promotion if you will!"

"Uh huh…"

I was completely taken aback.

As frivolous and flippant as Mèmè Oshino was, he was technically an expert in his field, and I was sure that even he would feel faint at the slapdash, perfunctory, and fantabulous logic of it.

Still, while I had no shortage of things to tell her, I was also in the position of having to worry at every waking moment about my attendance record, which meant I had to get to school on time. I kept our conversation to a couple of exchanges, said "Later," and hopped back on my bike seat.

That's when she told me.

"Um, Mister Araragi? I think I'm going to be wandering around this area for a while, so—"

This, from that girl.

"If you see me, please do speak to me."

So, yeah.

I guess it's quite a wonderful story.

Afterword

I felt like writing a regular afterword for once, so I'd like to take this chance to give something resembling commentary on the two tales included in this book. I will be going into details, so if any of you are reading this afterword before the main text, I'm sorry, but I suggest that you stop and come back after you've read the whole thing. Okay, what I felt like writing was just that stock introduction, and I won't actually be giving any commentary, but when you think about it, authors giving something like commentary on their own stories is no simple affair. People can't express their thoughts a hundred percent, and what does get expressed isn't going to make it across a hundred percent; in practice, you're at sixty percent for each if things go well, which would mean the audience of a work gets only thirty-six percent of what the author is thinking. The other sixty-four percent is made up of misunderstandings, so you often can't agree with more than half of what's being said when you read an author's own commentary. Like, hold on, that's what he was thinking? It's the so-called difficulty of communicating, but it's also an absolute fact that those misunderstandings spice things up in a good way. For example, when I suggest a book I love to people, I try to give an immersive account of a scene that moved me, but sometimes, upon rereading the book, I find out that the scene isn't there. At the end of the day, humans are unreliable creatures, so when we feel something, more

Note: *BAKEMONOGATARI* was initially serialized in the literary magazine *Mephisto* and later collected into two volumes in Japan, while this English edition is in three parts. In the original, this afterword refers to "three" rather than "two" tales and, in the penultimate paragraph, names the third chapter along with the first two.

than half of it is a misunderstanding, but maybe you shouldn't interpret it in a pessimistic way and instead look at it as the author or the story having the power to make you misunderstand. If you are a reader, I'm sure you've experienced looking back at a book that had an impact on you and realizing that it actually wasn't that big of a deal after all; and recommending a book that moved you in your teens to current teens, promising them that they'll love it, and not getting a great reaction, is something we all get a taste of. That's thanks to audience misunderstanding, or mental images if you want to put a better spin on it, and maybe instead of feeling let down, you ought to be giving thanks for the dreams the work allowed you to see. To add to that, there are those cases where whatever scene that wasn't there upon rereading crops up in a different book, but that's just my own sucky memory, for which no author or story is to be held responsible.

This book contains two tales that revolve around aberrations—would be a false statement. All I wanted to do was write a fun novel crammed full of stupid exchanges, and these tales are what happened when I did exactly that. Upon collecting them, we asked VOFAN to provide illustrations. If I may provide just a snippet of commentary, this all started from the syllogism that "*Tsundere* sounds kind of similar to *gerende*, a term derived from German that we use in Japan to mean 'skiing slope'" → "You can't talk about German and slopes without thinking of the word *pflugbogen,* a snowplough turn on skis" → "You can write *bogen* in Japanese using the characters for 'wildly inappropriate remark,' can't you." And so that was Hitagi Crab and Mayoi Snail, *BAKEMONOGATARI Part One.* You'll find even stupider exchanges in the next part, so please look forward to it.

A hundred percent of my gratitude to all of you out there who aren't me.

NISIOISIN